MILLS & BOON
100 YEARS
of pure reading pleasure

100 Reasons to Celebrate

We invite you to join us in celebrating
Mills & Boon's centenary. Gerald Mills and
Charles Boon founded Mills & Boon Limited
in 1908 and opened offices in London's Covent
Garden. Since then, Mills & Boon has become
a hallmark for romantic fiction, recognised
around the world.

We're proud of our 100 years of publishing
excellence, which wouldn't have been achieved
without the loyalty and enthusiasm of our
authors and readers.

Thank you!

Each month throughout the year there will
be something new and exciting to mark the
centenary, so watch for your favourite authors,
captivating new stories, special limited
edition collections…and more!

Dear Reader

Take a country girl and put her smack-bang in the centre of the city; that was my promise to you. And here she is! Country girl **Carly Tate**, the heroine of LAYING DOWN THE LAW, comes to town to join a high-powered legal firm. Introduce **Carly** to slick city lawyer **Lorenzo Domenico**, and watch those sparks fly!

Lorenzo is a hot Italian-American lawyer, over in the UK to introduce promising young lawyers to his scholarship programme… I said *scholarship programme*, **Lorenzo**! You naughty boy!

My inspiration for this book comes from a bona fide legal eagle, who confided some hair-raising experiences, and who better for me to share these with than you?

And this isn't the end of the story—**Carly Tate** has a sister. Look out for **Livvie** in my next Modern Heat book, coming soon.

Do visit my website at www.susanstephens.net, where I'm going to be running a feature on this book. You can find lots of extras on the site, such as contests and book news, as well as extracts. And don't forget to join my Birthday Babies on the 'Fun' page, to receive a card, button and goodies on your special day!

It's not often we can sit back and enjoy someone LAYING DOWN THE LAW… Let's make this time the exception.

Happy reading, everyone!

Susan

LAYING DOWN
THE LAW

BY
SUSAN STEPHENS

MILLS & BOON

Pure reading pleasure

First published in Great Britain 2008
Harlequin Mills & Boon Limited,
Eton House, 18-24 Paradise Road, Richmond, Surrey TW9 1SR

© Susan Stephens 2008

ISBN: 978 0 263 86368 0

Set in Times Roman 10½ on 12 pt.
171-0108-49015

Printed and bound in Spain
by Litografia Rosés, S.A., Barcelona

Susan Stephens was a professional singer before meeting her husband on the tiny Mediterranean island of Malta. In true Modern™ Romance style they met on Monday, became engaged on Friday, and were married three months after that. Almost thirty years and three children later, they are still in love. (Susan does not advise her children to return home one day with a similar story, as she may not take the news with the same fortitude as her own mother!)

Susan had written several non-fiction books when fate took a hand. At a charity costume ball there was an after-dinner auction. One of the lots, 'Spend a Day with an Author', had been donated by Mills & Boon® author Penny Jordan. Susan's husband bought this lot, and Penny was to become not just a great friend but a wonderful mentor, who encouraged Susan to write romance.

Susan loves her family, her pets, her friends and her writing. She enjoys entertaining, travel, and going to the theatre. She reads, cooks, and plays the piano to relax, and can occasionally be found throwing herself off mountains on a pair of skis or galloping through the countryside. Visit Susan's website: www.susanstephens.net—she loves to hear from her readers all around the world!

Look out for Susan's next Modern™ Romance, coming soon!

Recent books by the same author:

Modern Extra
DIRTY WEEKEND

Modern Romance
BOUGHT: ONE ISLAND, ONE BRIDE
ONE-NIGHT BABY

The Royal House of Niroli
EXPECTING HIS ROYAL BABY *Book 5*

For Wiggy

PROLOGUE

PARTIES BORED HIM. Office parties bored him most of all. But he'd been too busy to meet anyone in the hectic city chambers since he'd arrived in the country to head up an exchange programme between promising young lawyers in the UK and the US, and this was an opportunity to show his face, as well as to weigh up the raw material.

He paused in the entrance to the room. The reception was being held in honour of the latest judge on the local circuit to be elevated to the House of Lords. An uneasy silence had fallen and he knew immediately that something was wrong. The room was packed with the local legal aristocracy, together with a swarm of pupil barristers all hoping to be noticed. His gaze was drawn to the podium where a red-faced girl was struggling to make an introduction, while next to her stood the guest of honour, Judge Deadfast of Dearing. His Lordship appeared less than amused by the fact the girl appeared to have forgotten his name.

He held his breath as she tried again. *Judge Dredd?* It was time for him to step in….

The elderly man at Carly's side shifted impatiently as she tried again. 'And it is my great pleasure this evening to introduce

Judge…' Why had her mind chosen now to blank? Was it because the most incredible looking man she had ever seen in her life had just entered the room? Tall and fierce, with dark flashing eyes, he took in everything at a glance, including her red face, no doubt. With his tan, athletic build and thick, chocolate-brown hair, he was the quintessential Latin lover made flesh. While she was the quintessential fat girl battling to introduce a geriatric judge with eyebrows that badly needed shearing.

No wonder she'd lost her audience! Who wouldn't prefer to look at that gorgeous man?

Would she be defeated? Sucking in a deep breath, she tried again. 'Ladies and gentlemen—'

Response: nil. Humiliation: a bottomless pit.

She was a back-room girl, not an MC. But if she hoped to pursue her career at the bar and become an effective advocate she had to get over her stage fright fast. But now it was too late! The cavalry had arrived in the form of the man with more testosterone flying off him than sparks off a Catherine wheel.

A path formed in front of him as he strode across the room. 'Ladies and gentlemen,' he said, smiling confidently at his audience as he rescued the microphone. 'My apologies for being late…' He wasn't late of course, but no one knew that, did they?

He turned his charm on the judge next, keeping the microphone close to his lips. He could feel the rustle of interest in the room, the shower of pheromones in the air. He could also feel the abject misery of the girl who had failed, but he'd see to her later.

'Your Lordship, what an honour…' He continued in this vein until the apoplectic look on His Lordship's face had paled into his usual sepulchral pallor.

He stood back well pleased with his performance as the

grimly smiling judge left the podium to be toadied by his colleagues. Courting judges was his area of expertise; courting women, his passion. His spirited Italian mother had taught him that keeping women happy was fundamental to life. He had since learned that it was fundamental to his sanity. The red-faced girl was next in line for some TLC, but not before he'd won back her audience.

'My Lords, ladies and gentlemen… Some appreciation, if you please, for my learned colleague.' As he spoke he laid a protective arm over the culprit's shoulders and drew her forward. 'Who amongst us would have made the connection between our honoured guest Judge Deadfast of Dearing and that legendary comic-strip character Judge Joe Dredd, law enforcement *par excellence?*' He paused to allow the mood against the young woman under his protection to change. He had His Lordship's interest now. 'And let us not forget,' he added, raising his hands to silence the oohs and aahs of understanding rippling through his audience, 'that Judge Joe Dredd has the power to arrest, sentence, and even execute criminals on the spot. So I advise prudence tonight…' As His Lordship led the laughter, he relaxed, job done. 'Enjoy the rest of your evening, everyone!'

He turned to rescue his charge and found her gone. His mouth firmed when he spotted her at the bar.

She knocked back a second glass of wine, but nothing helped. She was over; finished. She wasn't a natural party animal, or speech-giver. Perhaps that was why her fellow pupil barristers had set her up by making her the compere…

As she picked up the wine bottle to pour herself some more, he made his move. Realising he was coming over she fired red and turned away, but not before he'd had a chance to assess the voluptuous figure. It appealed to his Latin soul, like the tilt of her chin and the abundance of Titian hair. Those were the points in her favour. On the reverse side of the coin she had the fashion sense of a—

Of an Englishwoman, he reminded himself as she glanced around to see how close he was.

She gasped to find him right behind her. 'I'm really, *really* grateful,' she blurted, drawing his attention to her wine-dampened lips. 'I don't know what came over me…'

She gulped as he took the wineglass out of her hand. 'Thanks for rescuing the situation. Can't imagine why you did it,' she finished awkwardly.

Chivalry would sound outdated to her, and he'd moved on in any case to urges and fantasies that had yet to be explored. His body, like his mind, was meant to be used. Years of study hadn't robbed him of the need to express himself physically, hence the workouts, tarmac, the gym, the sparring he indulged in twice a week. 'Think nothing of it,' he said, pouring her a glass of water. 'Here, drink this—you'll feel better in a minute.'

'Thank you,' she said, sipping demurely.

Dio! She was a contradiction. In unguarded moments her green eyes flashed fire, which gave him a hint of the busy thoughts beneath her frumpy exterior, and now he was close enough he could see her skin had the translucency of delicate porcelain. She might be considered gauche and awkward compared to the polish of the other girls in the room, but she had his attention. Taking the wine bottle she thought she had so cleverly hidden behind the punch bowl, he replaced it in the ice bucket where it belonged. 'I think you've had enough. It doesn't do to blunt the senses…'

His gravelly voice made her toes curl. He was so gorgeous. She had no coping strategies for a man with the body of a kick boxer dressed by Savile Row. Which hardly mattered. With his stubble-darkened face and commanding manner he could have any woman in the room. He would pour himself a drink, give her one of those dangerous half smiles, and walk away.

How did she know this? Because she had dressed carefully so as not to draw attention to herself, just as every other woman present had dressed to impress, and now she should get out of his way and spare herself the indignity of being asked to move. Unfortunately her feet refused to agree with this proposition and remained where they were. Glaring at them, she noticed his feet: shoe size large. She blanked out the obvious correlation to other parts of his anatomy.

As he flipped back his jacket to slip a hand in his pocket, he raised the line of one trouser leg enough to display the most extraordinary socks. A man in a traditional three-piece suit wearing crazy-coloured socks? Which said what about the workings in his head?

'Feeling better now?' Dark eyes probed deep, and the voice that went with them was intriguingly foreign: mid-Atlantic with a dash of chilli. He was waiting for her to say something, but her quickness of mind—the only worthwhile attribute she possessed—deserted her. All she could think was, You don't normally look at teeth and think, Bite me. But this man's teeth were very white, and very strong, and something in his mocking expression promised a very pleasurable nip indeed. He had the sexiest lips on earth, and his eyes…were expressive pools of wicked thoughts and sardonic humour; perfect.

But who was he? She was a pupil barrister in this busy city chambers, a freckle-faced country bumpkin with a lively interior mind, but the man towering over her was film-star perfect. 'Are you Italian?' It was the best she could come up with going on nothing more than his looks.

'Italian American,' he said, staring at her empty wineglass. 'I don't think you like parties any more than I do. Am I right?' He didn't wait for her answer. Taking hold of her arm, he drew her across the room, guiding her in and out of the alcohol-fuelled mayhem with an arm outstretched in front of her face.

To protect her?

No one had ever done that before. Everyone assumed she could look after herself. As they should; she was big and capable, but this was nice for a change.

As they walked she worked out that, as a stranger in town, he must want her to point him in the direction of the nearest taxi rank. But then he tested this assumption, taking her past the elevators and heading for the offices. She ran out of feasible alternatives as to what would happen next. And okay, maybe she would regret this in the morning, but tomorrow was another day…

'This office is being used as a cloakroom, I believe.' Trying the door, he held it open for her.

She stared at him blankly.

'You do have a coat, don't you? It's cold outside…'

All he wanted to do was help her on with her coat? That lively interior mind had let her down badly this time! 'You're assuming I'm ready to go—'

'Aren't you?'

Of course she was, but was that an invitation to leave with him? Her heart started thundering even though she doubted it.

'Shall I call a taxi for you?'

Not an invitation! 'It's only walking distance to my flat.'

'Are you sure?' He dipped his head to give her the type of stare a ringside doctor might give a boxer he suspected of being punch drunk.

'Absolutely sure…' The punch had been good, come to think of it. She'd made it herself to an old family recipe, and in hindsight perhaps the glasses of white wine on top of it had been a mistake. She tapped her foot, starting to feel uncomfortable beneath the scrutiny of a man who had taken grooming to new heights—six feet two or thereabouts, she guessed. 'Something wrong?' She grabbed her coat.

'Not at all. I just think you've had rather a lot to drink.'

'Are you judging me?'

The raised brow and almost-smile were the signal for her heartbeat to go crazy. 'Well, if you don't mind…' She stared pointedly at the door. He was way out of her league, so there was no point in prolonging the agony.

'Of course…' With a mocking bow, he stood aside.

Who was that man? she wondered again. Crunching frost beneath her boots, Carly realised his socks were the only clue she'd come away with. They'd been extraordinary: bright green with a motif of red boxing gloves, garnished with the badge of some club he must belong to… Which made sense when you considered the evidence—there was nothing soft about him—so maybe he was just that: a particularly desirable kick boxer with a keen sense of style. Whatever the case, she was too busy developing her career to think about men.

Her body disagreed. Her body wanted things her mind would never allow. Fortunately, reason prevailed. If his intentions had been dishonourable when he had led her by the hand towards that darkened office she would have pulled back. She would never have given way to lust.

Never.

Never!

Oh, all right then, she might have done.

Fortunately the opportunity to test her resolve would never arise. She might not be Brain of Britain, but she was bright enough to know the ugly duckling never got the prince.

CHAPTER ONE

YOU COULD HEAR a pin drop in the lecture theatre. A fly on the wall might say the man teaching law could only be Italian. One thing was certain. With his striking Latin looks, impeccable tailoring and autocratic stare, Lorenzo Domenico could hold an audience spellbound. Women had stampeded the law school to secure a place in his class and on this first morning they outnumbered the men ten to one. Lorenzo Domenico might be new in town, but he was already a legend.

Lorenzo paced as he spoke, pausing occasionally to shoot an impatient glance at his adoring audience. He wanted to check if they were listening. He intended his standards to be the highest on the faculty. He'd worked hard, and now he expected that same application from his students. He tested them constantly, often in the most unexpected ways. In Lorenzo's opinion anyone who possessed a photographic memory could pass an exam, but could they fathom the intricacies of law and come to the best result for their client? He called it lateral thinking. Some of his students called it unreasonable; they were the ones who didn't make it through the course.

Along with heading up the scholarship programme he had agreed to mentor a pupil barrister at the top flight chambers in the city where he had tenancy. Multitasking was his speciality, intolerance of those who couldn't keep up his only failing—though his adoring Italian mother would have disagreed, and persuaded him he had no failings. Lorenzo smiled. Mama was always right.

Pausing mid-stride, he checked his register. There was someone missing. Instinct made him glance out of the window. He tensed. 'Will you excuse me? That wasn't a question,' he added as a groan of disappointment rose in the lecture theatre. He was already halfway through the door. The student who was late had just slammed her rusty old bike into his pristine Alfa Romeo.

'You cannot wipe it off,' he roared, exiting the outer doors like an avenging angel. He had arrived just in time to see the young woman's pink tongue flick out to wet her finger.

'It's a very small scratch,' she explained, her green eyes rounding with sincerity. 'Oh…' The blood drained from her face. 'Hello…'

He stood motionless, taking in the facts. Whichever way he looked at it, this was bad.

Carly paled as her mind absorbed the information: Carly Tate crashes into the car of her senior tutor Lorenzo Domenico on her first morning in his class. Not only that, she'd just received a letter to say he'd been appointed her pupil master in chambers, plus he chaired the committee for the Unicorn scholarship; the scholarship she had promised her parents. How much better could it get?

No prizes for guessing his thoughts: Oh, no, not her again! Shortly followed by, Do I associate with failure? She could hardly pretend the fiasco last night had escaped his notice. And now this! To distract them both she pointed to the damage on his car. 'You can see how small it is…' But now she looked again the gouge seemed to have grown.

'Small?' he said with a curl of his lip.

No wonder she hadn't recognised him last night. Since arriving in the UK Lorenzo Domenico had barely settled long enough to register a shadow. Winning a no-hoper case in his first month in town had raised his profile to the extent that the clerks who managed his diary were looking at a twelve-month waiting list. Lorenzo wouldn't be returning home any time soon—or ever, if the rumours were to be believed—so it was time to build bridges. Fast. 'I'm really sorry about your car—'

'You will be.' He cut her off crisply.

He hadn't been dubbed the scourge of the courts for nothing. What a perfect start to her scholarship hopes! Her fellow pupils had all landed some elderly old duffer who schooled them in an atmosphere of calm and dusty academe, while she had scored Torquemada, Chief Inquisitor.

She had been so sure she could deal with a man like Lorenzo Domenico when she had first read the letter, in fact she'd been rather thrilled, but there was a huge gulf between the written word and the man standing in front of her now. And ominously his socks were tartan, suggesting he was poised to dance a jig on the grave of her ambition. But she wasn't going down without a fight. 'I think you'll find that the scratch will polish out—'

'Do not presume to practise your advocacy skills on me, Ms Tate.' His eyes turned cold. 'Take a look at my car.'

'Very nice—'

'I mean the damage to my car, Ms Tate. Look at that. If you examine it closely you will see that the scratch will not polish out.'

She shook her head like a wayward pony, sending shimmering auburn curls flying round her shoulders. He admired the hair, but it distracted him. She was a student and his sole purpose in life was to whip her into shape.

'I can hardly see it,' she protested.

Her determination to fight pleased him. He liked a fight. 'And a *very small* scratch on a hired car will affect my deposit how, *Ms* Tate?' He would drive her hard like all his students. Time was short, and they had to learn more than the letter of the law, they had to absorb an immeasurable lexicon of nuance and interpretation. If they weren't up to it, it was better to find out now. 'Come on, come on,' he goaded her. 'Aren't you supposed to be a lawyer?'

'I am a lawyer,' she retorted, holding his gaze.

Another rush of pleasure hit him. He didn't want his students to fail; he wanted them all to excel—even this sorry excuse of an MC. 'You may be a lawyer one day,' he said, 'but not yet. And if you're late for my class again, you never will be. You will fail the course and lose your chance to be considered for the scholarship.'

'I'm really sorry—'

'Sorry doesn't cut it with me, Ms Tate.'

'*Very* sorry…'

She raised her head to confront him in a way that almost made up for her blunders, because now he caught a glimpse of a strong inner core. She would need that when she stood up in court. Her face was easy on the eye too. Though not glamorous or attractive to him, she had a fresh-faced look he found appealing. After all the painted sophisticates he'd been introduced to on the so-called social scene she was a refreshing change.

And then there were his students. His impression of them to date was that the females were slightly less good-looking than the men, which, as a serial heterosexual, was a serious concern to him.

He'd read the report on Carly Tate, as he had read the reports on all his students. She was the brightest of the bright,

but was she right for law? That was what he meant to find out.
But if she was going to work with him she'd have to clean up
her act. For instance, what was she wearing? A jacket with
bald cuffs, which she had teamed with ripped and faded jeans,
and on her feet something that looked as if she had made them
herself out of a couple of hides and a yard of ribbon.

She hadn't made the slightest effort to impress, which
insulted him. She looked as if she'd just climbed out of bed,
which enraged him. Women should be chaste and available
and waiting for him to notice them. His eyes darkened as he
pictured his ideal woman waking slowly and languorously
with the memories of the previous night still heavy in her
eyes, and on her plump, perfectly formed lips...

Why was he staring at her lips? Did she have a milk mous-
tache?

Clearing her throat, Carly made that her excuse for swiping
a hand across her mouth.

Charming! Such grace and style, these Englishwomen. 'So,'
he rapped, staring at her, before turning to look at the one
thing that could distract an Italian man from thoughts of
family, football, fashion or fornication: his car. 'What do you
intend to do about the damage and my claim for reparation?'

She recited the relevant passages of law to him flawlessly,
but then, remembering the preliminary notes he'd circulated
prior to the course, he realised what a good teacher he was.
'I see you've read my notes.'

'Of *course* I have,' she said, pinking up again.

'I'll leave you to report the damage, in that case,' he said
coldly. 'Arrange for repairs and keep me informed...'

He was pleased to see how well she responded to instruction. But as he turned to go he could have sworn she clicked

her heels. He almost swung round to challenge her, but then contented himself with the thought that dealing with trouble-makers was something he excelled at. He loved trouble; his career had been built on it.

Reaching the entrance to the building, he stopped and turned abruptly. Her cheeks flamed red as he fixed a stony stare upon her face. Pleased with the effect, he moved in for the kill. 'As you've already missed the main thrust of my lecture I'd like you to return home and dress for court.'

Her face brightened. 'Court?'

There wasn't a student barrister alive who didn't ache to ease the tedium of study with some real-life drama in the courtroom. 'Yes, court,' he said evenly. 'I left my wig and gown there. You can collect them for me.'

It amused him to see her eyes fire bullets at him while her face remained carefully blank. He revised his opinion of her again—upwards. She'd make a great lawyer if she possessed the will to do so. But he hadn't finished with her yet. 'You can't go to court as my representative dressed like that.'

'Oh, don't worry about me,' she said, starting to gather her spilled belongings. 'This suit will brush down fine.' Retrieving some rag from the gutter, she shook it out.

'In case it's escaped your notice, Ms Tate, that suit is covered in mud, and you work under me now.' An unfortunate turn of phrase, perhaps, but too late to call it back. He added some iron to the mix. 'I forbid you to go to court dressed like that. What will people think?'

'That I can't afford cleaning bills…?'

There was such an expression of innocence on her face he considered his grounds for launching a rebuke uncertain. Everyone knew that pupil barristers existed largely on fresh air and the charity of their parents, plus her face was already flaming with mortification, and his intention had never been to crush her. While he contemplated this she rallied. Angling her chin, she waited, as if expecting him to pat her on the head for arriving at the right answer. He knew her type immediately. She was the child who had always known the right answer in class, and who had shot up her hand before anyone else had a chance to, oblivious to how unpopular that made her. He could only contrast that with his own childhood when he'd only had to burp for everyone to applaud him in breathless admiration. Nonetheless, he had to set her right. 'No, Ms Tate. They will not think that. They will think you so rushed this morning you didn't have a chance to look in the mirror. Do you want to leave an impression of incompetence behind you? No, I didn't think so.'

Inconvenient images invaded Carly's mind as Lorenzo delivered his ultimatum, of flinging the wretched suit at his feet and jumping on it. Did he think bespoke suits like his grew on trees? Did he think parking across the cycle path was a good idea? But these images were swiftly followed by her parents' anxious faces. She couldn't let them down, and while there was life left in her scholarship hopes she had not the slightest intention of doing so.

CHAPTER TWO

'AND YOUR SECOND TASK for today, Ms Tate…'

They were in Lorenzo's office. He was seated; she was standing in front of him like a recalcitrant child. She kept her expression carefully neutral. It wasn't that she had suddenly become immune to the power storm swirling round Lorenzo, but the fact that her feet were killing her. She had made a real effort to conform to the image she imagined he would have in mind for a successful female applicant for the Unicorn scholarship, and if that involved wearing the type of heels that were almost impossible to come by for farmyard feet, then that was what she would do.

'You're a front runner for the scholarship,' he said. 'You do know that, don't you?'

Say yes, and be damned for complacency, or say no and appear a wuss. She decided not to comment and straightened her back, assuming what she hoped he would take for a determined stance. And while she did that she gave full rein to her lust. Playing poker face was an area in which she excelled.

'You do realise what's hanging on your performance over the next few weeks?'

She might have known Lorenzo wouldn't give up until he had forced an answer out of her. Thinking about her parents made a clean sweep of her mind and the lust. Her parents had talked of nothing but the scholarship for months now, and both the bridge club and golf club were waiting agog for news of her latest triumph, apparently.

'Ms Tate.' Lorenzo snapped her out of the reverie.

'Yes?' She held back on the temptation to salute.

'Do I have your total commitment to this project?'

'One hundred per cent.'

'Good.' He relaxed a little, which was enough to give her a grandstand view of his socks…as well as just a hint of the tanned and deliciously muscular hairy legs above them. Her cheeks fired up like warning beacons when he caught her staring.

'Something wrong?' he said.

'No…of course not—'

'That outfit won't do,' he said, turning his attention to her clothes. He wrinkled his nose as he scrutinised the same suit he'd seen lying in the gutter. She had sponged it down since then with a pungent though effective mix of hot water and vinegar. She had wanted to look her best for this momentous first one-on-one meeting with her pupil master, except, of course, this wasn't their first one-on-one encounter. 'I'm sorry about your car—'

'Never mind that now,' he said impatiently. 'I expect you to deal with that in your own time. This is my time, and while you're under my tutelage I expect you to prove you're a lawyer worth sorting out.'

'Oh, I am,' she said eagerly. Her cheeks fired as her body entertained some frenzied notions involving Lorenzo sorting her out. 'What I mean is, I won't disappoint you—' The fire in her cheeks went up a notch when she noticed his interested gaze lingering on her breasts. Her suit jacket wouldn't close over them and was hanging open, revealing a paper-thin shirt that had seen much better days. 'I'm ready to be sorted out,' she blurted recklessly. 'And I promise to try and find some-thing more suitable to wear.' As she spoke she clutched the edges of her jacket in a last-ditch attempt to make it close.

'Be sure that you do.'

Carly couldn't tell if Lorenzo was amused or angry as he turned his attention to the documents on his desk, but now it was her turn to study him. The fine wool of his dark, bespoke suit clung attractively to his powerful frame, and she guessed he would have to have suits made for him as the spread of his shoulders was so wide—

Looking up, he snapped, 'I thought I told you to go home and change?'

Change into what? Ally McBeal? She was wearing a thrift-shop find, and going home to change her clothes would involve donning another thrift-shop find. She had to come clean and explain. 'I would, but—'

'But?' Lorenzo let the word hang like a dead rat. 'No excuses, Ms Tate. If you intend to succeed you must do what I say, when I say it.'

Had she signed up to join the army? And what would it take to soften that firm mouth?

'If you have difficulty following a simple instruction perhaps we'd better sort that out before we go any further,' Lorenzo rapped, jolting her back to full attention. Holding up a list with the logo of the Unicorn scholarship printed prominently on the top of the sheet of paper, he said, 'If you're not willing to go the extra mile in every area of your professional life I think it better for both of us if I cross your name off this list now.'

'Are you threatening me?' She couldn't believe she'd said it, but something made her blunder on. 'Did you spare a thought for the consequences of parking your flashy new car across the cycle path? Or was it more important to leave a gleaming Alpha Romeo where you could admire it from the window? That way, I suppose, when the cogs of your students' minds failed to turn swiftly enough you'd got at least one piece of outstanding machinery to admire.'

'Finished?' Lorenzo demanded coolly. He shifted in his chair. 'Passion, Ms Tate. I like that in an advocate. But I'd also like you to consider the perils of over-larding your assertions when you're standing up in court.'

His eyes were like black diamonds, and the ice in his voice was a salutary reminder that Lorenzo Domenico had not risen to the top of the legal levee on a tide of emotion.

'Yes or no, Ms Tate?' he demanded, pen poised.

Her heart was racing. Her lips were parted…

She was aroused!

And not just aroused, she was thoroughly stirred up, which was unusual—no, make that unique! This unexpected confrontation with Lorenzo was rousing parts of her that had remained dormant for years. And at this, one of the most crucial moments in her life!

She had to get over it, and let her mind rule; her parents needed this. 'You can put your pen down,' she said with matching calm. 'I'm up to the challenge.'

If only Lorenzo didn't have quite such a direct and perceptive stare, but she had to be up to the challenge. She hadn't moved from a sleepy village—where her parents were pillars of the local community—to the city, only to fail them. Her goal was to make her parents proud, and if that meant jousting with Lorenzo like this then she would. She wanted the Unicorn scholarship more than anything. *Other than a hug sometimes*… 'You mentioned a second task?' she prompted, rattling her brain cells into order.

'I'd like you to organise the Christmas party.'

The poisoned chalice! Her stomach clenched.

'The holidays come around each year, Ms Tate,' he said

briskly. 'There's no need to look so startled. I have been informed that we host a spectacular Christmas party each year, and I'm offering you the chance to make this year's the best. I would have thought you would be grateful for an opportunity to shine.' He said this wearily. 'You have four days,' he added in a harder tone.

Four days? He made it sound as if four days was a generous amount of time in which to achieve the impossible. Lorenzo had unerringly settled on the one task for which her finely-tuned brain was most ill equipped. She was a swot, not a party planner. She collected scholarships like other people collected golf trophies. But Lorenzo was right in saying this was a chance to impress, if not the chance she had been hoping for. She didn't have sufficient polish to lay on something grand for a group of sophisticated lawyers.

But polish could be acquired, Carly reminded herself, whereas ambition had been stamped on her forehead at birth. She was going to nail this.

'If you don't feel up to the task I can always ask someone else.'

'That won't be necessary,' she assured him. 'I can handle it.' If he'd asked her to walk up and down Oxford Street with a sandwich-board on her back advertising ambulance-chasing services, she'd do that too. All it took to cement her determination in place was the thought of her mother's face if she failed, or her father's friends shaking their heads behind his back, if she returned home empty-handed. She had to win Lorenzo's respect somehow if she was going to land the wretched scholarship. She was going to grasp this nettle and shake it in his face. She was going to put on the best Christmas party there'd ever been.

Somehow.

'Are you sure?' he pressed, staring at her intently. 'You can't afford to get this wrong, Ms Tate.'

Thanks for the confidence boost! 'I'm positive. You've got nothing to worry about.' She tipped her chin and found a confident, businesslike smile to match the brave words. She had already fathomed how she was going to turn what her mother was sure to see as a menial task into a positive: Lorenzo had *entrusted* her with the task of organising the most important chambers event of the year. The fact that you didn't need an honours degree from Cambridge to do that would never occur to her mother.

She hoped.

'Very well, then…' Lorenzo's dark eyes glinted as the challenge began. 'Well? What are you waiting for? You'd better make a start.'

It was the ultimate test for Carly. He doubted she had ever attended the type of party where networking and point-scoring were a given, champagne and caviare just a starting point. He wanted to push her; he wanted to find out about those hidden depths. Would she ring a party planner and take the easy way out? He'd known that to happen in the past. It usually ended in disaster with the student forced to ring Mummy and Daddy to provide extra funds when they realised how little they would be receiving from him.

Yes, this was one of his favourite tests.

Back in the cubby-hole that passed for her office, Carly reviewed her position. Planning a sophisticated party took her so far out of her comfort zone her first inclination was to laugh hysterically. Carly Tate, the girl least likely to party, was now expected to arrange one!

Her mother expressed serious doubts when she rang up for advice. 'If only your sister were there to help you…' But Livvie wouldn't be there to help…

She felt a pang as she thought about her sister. Livvie had a talent for bringing people together and making them smile and could sprinkle fairy dust over any gathering. But, clueless or not, this was her party. It was just one more mountain to climb. And climb it she would.

Dusting off the crampons of her ambition, she got to work. The phrase 'party planner' sang in her mind as she spotted the telephone directory, but then remembering the tone of Lorenzo's instructions, she changed her mind. He had asked her to organise the party; he hadn't asked her to delegate. This was just another of his little tests, Carly concluded, determined to play Lorenzo at his own game.

Playing Lorenzo at his own game involved seeing him again during his working day, and he didn't welcome her interruption. But he could turn on the hard stare all he liked, she wasn't going anywhere until she had the information she needed. 'I must know more before I can start to plan.' She used a firm voice to distract him from the papers he was studying.

'For instance?' His gazed pierced her.

'Budget?' She held her ground even though Lorenzo was so tensely poised behind his desk he looked like a cougar about to pounce. 'I must know the budget I'll be working to…' It was hard to block out images of chocolate fountains and multiple crates of champagne. Having perused the guest list, she knew a number of eminent QCs and judges from other chambers would be attending, and they'd expect the best. Her confidence was growing by the minute. Party planning wasn't so bad. It was just a question of making lists and sourcing suppliers—

'Budget?' Lorenzo barked, cutting her off mid self-congratulation. 'Slim, Ms Tate!'

Was that an instruction? She sucked in her stomach, just in case.

Lorenzo fixed her with a basilisk stare. 'Bring every quotation to me. Don't agree to anything without my direct permission. Do I make myself clear, Ms Tate?' His voice had dropped to a penetrating whisper.

Crystal. She would use lawyer's discretion, which meant that anything she could get away with, she would. Unfortunately she didn't have such an immediate answer to the irresponsible behaviour of her body, which was responding frantically to the stern note in Lorenzo's voice. She liked that. She liked it a lot. Probably because she could see all sorts of erotic possibilities in her mind's eye. She gave a brisk nod to cover for her abstraction as her fantasies played out.

Lorenzo scribbled something on a pad, which he handed over to her. 'Here's your guideline spending limit…'

Taking the paper from him, Carly read it and tried not to gulp. Her scholarship was definitely teetering in the balance, not on a champagne fountain, as she had hoped, but on a beer mug and a plate of curling sandwiches. She could forget the graceful twelve-foot tree, tastefully decorated with colour-coordinated baubles and flashing lights—clear, of course, she knew that much. With the budget Lorenzo had just handed her she'd be lucky if she could afford a pot-plant and a torch.

'If the task's too much for you—' he began wearily.

'Not at all,' she interrupted him.

'Then, if you don't mind…' He stared pointedly at the pile of papers on his desk.

'Of course,' she said coolly. 'I'll start working on it right away.'

When the door had shut behind her he sat back. Would she crumble? He hoped not. Closing his eyes briefly, he thought he could detect the faint aroma of wildflowers in the air. Ms

Tate was proving a lot harder to blank from his mind than he had anticipated. And his body would have some striking images to dip into as well if she didn't find a suit jacket that fitted. The end result was he found it impossible to concentrate.

Springing up, he paced the room. So what if the task he had handed her was impossible? A working lawyer rarely encountered anything ordinary or expected in court. He wanted to see how she reacted, how she thought on her feet when she was up against a wall...

He had to shake his head to drive away that disturbing image before he could progress his thoughts. Her development as a lawyer was under his command. On paper she was the front runner for the scholarship, but was it enough? She was a hopeless public speaker, which put her future as an effective advocate in jeopardy. And maybe she did have the best possible paper qualifications, but was her memory suspect? Was it possible she had forgotten what was happening tonight? She certainly hadn't mentioned it. Yet she faced a crucial test. Had it slipped her mind? And if it had, what could possibly have distracted her to that extent?

Lorenzo. Lorenzo. Lorenzo. Why couldn't she get him out of her head? He seemed to have taken up permanent residence in there, Carly thought, raking her hair in frustration. And it was imperative she concentrate on the task at hand. Four days was hardly enough time to organise a cup of tea in this place, let alone a full-blown Christmas party!

Chewing the top of her pencil, she wracked her brain for that one brilliant idea that would astound everyone.

And failed.

The only clearly focused thought in her head was the knowledge that Lorenzo would never look at her in the way her body thought he should. Why would he, when he was older and worldly-wise, wildly successful and far better looking? Face it, he wouldn't, and that was that.

Lorenzo rasped his beard with one firm thumb pad. He was still pondering Carly's inexplicable lapse of memory. Tonight was the Grand Court, a legal ceremonial notorious as the killing ground of pupils. He would have thought she'd be prepared for it. The Grand Court was geared to weed out the weaker members of the bar before they had chance to gain a foothold in the profession. It went without saying that any pupil of his would succeed and pass the test with flying colours—and without any prompting from the sidelines. But on this occasion he wondered if there might be too large a gulf between his expectation and Carly's performance. He refused to believe she could simply forget, just as he refused to give her an unfair advantage over the other pupils. He felt a little reassured when her determined face flashed into his mind. Of course she had everything in hand. If she hadn't she'd be squashed like a bug.

Back in her cubby-hole Carly sat with her head in her hands. There wasn't a chance she could organise the type of party Lorenzo was expecting on the measly budget he had allowed. Hard work wasn't enough in this instance. She needed a miracle.

Her head bounced as her eyes fired with inspiration. *Of course!* Why hadn't she thought of it sooner? She didn't have to compete with some glitz and glamour event. All she had to do was land on something bold and different, something novel and unexpected—

And hope she didn't fall flat on her face.

CHAPTER THREE

SLURPING COFFEE without tasting it, Carly continued scribbling notes. The ideas were coming thick and fast now, and driving her hard towards party nirvana was the knowledge that she had less than a week to put everything in place…food, drink, music, decorations, dress—

Dress!

Pushing back from the desk, she yelped in alarm. How could she have forgotten tonight? How could she have forgotten a night as crucial to her career as the Grand Court?

Lorenzo. She blamed him entirely.

He had shot everything from her brain in less time than it took to…

Clear your mind, Carly.

Pressing her fingertips against her temples, she battled hard to erase images of her stern pupil master performing all sorts of pre-sentence examinations on her all too eager and totally irresponsible body.

And failed.

She was doing quite a lot of that recently.

But the Lorenzo effect was a concern for another day. The Grand Court was so important to her future she couldn't believe it had slipped her mind. *Nothing* slipped her mind *ever*.

Before Lorenzo.

The Grand Court was a rite of passage for every pupil barrister, and as such should have taken precedence over everything. And she didn't have a thing to wear. If there'd been room in her cramped cubby-hole she would have paced up and down. It was too dreadful to contemplate. All the senior lawyers, including Lorenzo, would be attending; there was no getting out of it. And she hadn't given it a thought.

He'd known that and let her stew?

His sardonic face flashed into her mind. Of course he had.

So she would fight fire with fire. The Christmas party would just have to take a back seat until tomorrow. If she failed the Grand Court she wouldn't make the Christmas party anyway, Carly thought, grimacing. Plus the golf and bridge clubs would be forced to fly their flags at half-mast, which was out of the question.

Settling back down, she tried to remain calm. The Grand Court was no picnic—unless you took into account the bread rolls flying your way if you messed up. The ceremony was held annually in the vaulted dining hall of one of the ancient Inns of Court. If you failed the test you were a laughing stock, and if you succeeded you could expect no praise. Following centuries of tradition the senior lawyers were expected to heckle the pupils as they stood to make their formal application to join the circuit. There were no rules, no quarter given, and only last year a judge's daughter had been sick in her own handbag. She told herself to concentrate on the positives.

All one of them.

Her middle name was Viola, like Shakespeare's heroine in *Twelfth Night*. The play had first been performed in 1602 in the very same hall where the Grand Court was held. What more mojo did she need? Everything would be fine.

Hopefully.

All she had to do was stand up and state her name, along with the date of her call, and the ancient Inn that had called her to the bar. After that, she just had to declare her wish to join the circus—

Circuit, Carly corrected herself grimly.

A slip like that could cost her her career. If she stumbled over the words, tradition demanded she start her little speech all over again, which was when the seniors' fun began. It was their task to shout her down, drown her out, and ultimately destroy her.

Calm, Carly commanded herself a second time, sucking in a deep, steadying breath. Everything would go to plan, but she must leave no stone unturned, which brought her thoughts full circle to the question of her outfit for the occasion. Fortunately, she had a secret weapon…

Madeline Du Pre, the most senior pupil in chambers, was Carly's elder by three years. Madeline was the recognised expert in fashion by virtue of a stint at a Swiss finishing school. Rumour had it that Madeline had been forced to repeat her first six months of training several times due to… Well, no one really knew, and Madeline wasn't telling, but the pupil master in charge of broadening her experience, one Judge Roger Warrington, never visited Madeline's office unaccompanied these days.

Madeline the modiste if not the modest, Carly thought as she rapped smartly on Madeline's door.

Carly didn't have long to wait for Madeline's verdict.

'Black? Are you mad?'

'Black's safe,' Carly protested. 'Legal-black is practically a definition,' she pointed out. 'In fact it should be a colour in the paint box. I can see it now—black, with a silvering of dust, and a touch of green mould… Don't look at me like that, Madeline. You know as well as I do that wearing black will take you through anything.'

'Except a wedding.' Madeline sniffed. 'For you…' cocking her head to one side, she gave Carly a long, considering look '…it has to be orange.'

'Orange?' Carly's eyes widened as she pictured her flame-coloured hair framed in orange. 'Are you sure?'

'Quite sure… Orange will be perfect with your colouring.'

It was important to get this right, and Madeline's scarlet talons were already drumming the desk.

'If you really think so…' Carly's voice trailed away as a horror snap in some down-market journal flew into her mind. There would be a banner heading with her looking fat, proclaiming, ORANGE JUSTICE!

But Madeline was already leading her by the arm towards the door…

'Stop worrying. Orange is absolutely your colour,' Madeline soothed. 'You mustn't even think of wearing black. You can only wear black when you've been accepted by the Grand Court. You'll cause an uproar if you go against tradition, Carly. Now, fortunately I can help you out. There's a fabulous second-hand designer clothes place, just about half a mile from here. I saw a dress in their window this morning that would be perfect for you. I even have their card…'

She handed it over and Carly read, 'One Starry Night: Model gowns by Madame Xandra… Available to hire, or to buy…'

'Thank you,' Carly said, frowning uncertainly.

It wasn't that Carly was fat, Madame Xandra explained helpfully, it was just that ball gowns were meant to fit snugly.

Which was all right for Madame Xandra, Carly thought mutinously, since she was thread-thin. Viewing her red face in the mirror, she knew she couldn't possibly hold her breath like this all evening, but on the other hand she couldn't bear the humiliation of trying to squeeze her plumpness into any more undersized Barbie-frocks. 'Yes, this one is absolutely perfect,' she said in answer to Madame Xandra's pained look.

The day could only get better, Carly told herself firmly, taking a final look at herself before setting out. Somehow she had managed to shoehorn her way into The Dress unaided, but she wasn't keen on looking too closely at the bulges of flesh fighting with an abundance of closely draped tangerine satin. The only good thing about it was that the gown seemed to answer the 'formal' dress stipulation on the gilt-edged invitation.

Edgily humming a song, she attempted last-minute to twirl her abundant red hair into some sort of sensible and therefore noticeably more compact style. She tried telling herself that everything was going to be all right, but that didn't work. How could it when she felt like a galleon under sail, roped, braced and mortally constricted? It was hardly the mood of choice for a night out in the spotlight!

Did the first person she had to see the moment she stepped down gingerly from the taxi have to be Lorenzo? And looking more like a film star than ever in his dark Alpaca coat, under which Carly knew he would be wearing a similarly impeccable tailored evening suit.

She stood for a moment to watch him greeting the other guests. He was so regal, and so confident of approval. And no wonder when he drew people to him like a magnet. Everyone wanted to bask in Lorenzo Domenico's darkly glittering glamour, no doubt hoping some of it would rub off on them…

The white silk scarf around his neck fascinated her. It was lifting in the breeze—not flying off as it would have done had she been wearing it, causing all sorts of hullabaloo, nor landing in his face and sticking on his lips, just…lifting.

Carly shut her mouth, conscious she was gawping. Her pupil master looked simply gorgeous with the wind ruffling his thick, dark hair. Where style was concerned Italians always got it right, she mused, unlike dumpy Englishwomen named Carly Tate, with her big feet and truly enormous breasts.

Lorenzo remained standing, a solitary figure, as the crowds peeled away. Staring up, he seemed transfixed by something. Following his gaze, she saw he was admiring the ancient buildings. She had forgotten how beautiful the Inns of Court were, but seeing them through Lorenzo's eyes was like seeing them anew. They were such totems to power, and such incredible monuments to the men who had designed and built them. Verging on Gothic with a special serenity all their own, they were truly awe-inspiring…

Carly shifted guiltily when, turning, Lorenzo noticed her. 'Carly,' he said, coming over. 'You're looking very—' The all-too-familiar ironic expression was firmly in place.

'Colourful?' she supplied, wanting the painful moment over with. She hadn't failed to notice as the crowds streamed past that everyone else was dressed in black, plus she was the only woman sporting a ball gown and showing her breasts. She had been set up, and it was too late to do anything about it. She just had to smile and get on with it.

'Are you ready for your ordeal?' Lorenzo murmured, trying very hard not to smile.

'You mean it hasn't started yet?'

Her dry comment unleashed something in him and he laughed. Unfortunately for her that sexy rumble had the same effect as a low-voltage charge to her most sensitive regions, which was the last thing required if she was to keep her wits about her tonight.

'Shall we go inside?' he suggested, offering his arm.

Lorenzo was offering to escort her inside? Did the most lusted-after, successful lawyer in London really want to be seen with a country bumpkin dressed in an orange meringue, or was Lorenzo merely using her as a foil to make himself look better?

He hardly needed to do that, Carly concluded.

'Well?' he pressed, a suspicious tug appearing at one corner of his mouth. 'Are you coming inside?'

Her exhalation of breath was noisily ragged as she considered this suggestion.

'Carly?' He dipped his head to look her in the eyes. She didn't dare to breathe on him. But he wouldn't wait for ever. Her options were obvious—she could turn tail and run, or she could brave it out.

Walking in on Lorenzo's arm felt good. People stared. At him, of course, she knew that, but still it proved, if proof were needed, that the only accessory a girl really needed was a bedworthy man.

Standing beneath the brilliantly lit chandeliers, Carly felt her new-found confidence draining away. Everyone else looked so elegant, while she felt like an orange marker buoy set adrift in a sea of penguins.

'Shall I take your shawl?' Lorenzo suggested. 'It will be quite safe with my coat in the cloakroom,' he reassured when she hesitated.

But would she be safe? Carly wondered as he twitched the yards of fabric away. She needed something substantial to cover the acres of chest on show.

As Lorenzo strode away Carly noticed how the crowd parted for him. She would never be able to make the same sort of impact. In fact she noticed now that the space around her suggested people feared bad taste might be catching. She

was so wrapped up in humiliation she gasped out loud when
Lorenzo returned.

'I didn't mean to startle you.'

But his eyes were sparkling. No doubt he was already an-
ticipating the fun he was about to have at her expense.

'Which table are you sitting at? Haven't you checked?' he
added with a frown when she didn't answer.

Actually, no, she hadn't checked. She had been frozen to
the spot, too embarrassed to move and show herself and her
terrible dress off in the sombre gathering. 'No, I haven't
checked.'

'There's no need to raise your voice,' Lorenzo pointed out
smoothly. 'Why don't I take you now to find out where
you're sitting?'

'Because I don't need you to?' It was just a shame for the
sake of her defiance that her voice was trembling.

'Clearly you do, *Ms* Tate,' Lorenzo contradicted her with
a raised brow.

Staying hidden in the shadows held far more appeal than
making herself the subject of gossip on Lorenzo's arm as she
walked across the crowded ballroom, but what option did
she have when he had taken a firm hold of her?

Just as Carly had anticipated, everyone turned to stare, but
at her, this time—or, at least, at the orange meringue. 'This
is so kind of you, Lorenzo,' she ground out through gritted
teeth.

'Don't mention it,' he murmured in a sardonic tone, bringing his head close to hers. 'If I'd left you to your own devices
I imagine they would have been passing the port by the time
you found your table, and I don't want you to miss your slot
tonight. I'm *so* looking forward to it…'

Shaking her arm free, she walked ahead. Lorenzo could
suck all the rational thought out of your brain with a single

look, and she had no intention of being distracted by him tonight, or mocked. But, having escaped his protection, Carly became aware that she was getting even more amused looks. And no wonder when she was the only woman showing her breasts, and they were big, bouncing breasts that refused to be hidden. Right now they felt like barrage balloons beneath her rigidly corseted top. And it didn't help her confidence any to see Madeline du Pre sailing past in a sharp Armani suit!

Reaching the table plan, she stared up. Grinding her teeth so hard they almost chipped, she forced herself to concentrate as a sound of disappointment rang out somewhere close to her left ear.

'You're not sitting with me.'

Lorenzo's comment sent a buzz of awareness spinning down her spine. 'Are you disappointed?'

'Disappointed?' he said. 'Without eye protection I'll feel much safer observing you from a distance.'

She should have known taking on Lorenzo would end in tears. But perhaps tears wouldn't be stinging the backs of her eyes if she hadn't felt so ridiculous. 'You could have warned me about the black dress code.'

'And show favouritism to my own pupil?'

She held his gaze and hardened her heart. Would any of the seniors have finer feelings? No, they were here to have fun at their pupils' expense. Tipping her chin, she went for a forceful gesture that was meant to demonstrate her nonchalant acceptance of her fate, but which unfortunately lifted her breasts clear of the constraining bodice. It was harder to appear defiant now while she was hastily stuffing them back in, and, to make matters worse, Lorenzo showed no intention of turning away as any gentleman should.

'I'm impressed,' he murmured, taking a leisurely ocular stroll down the Grand Canyon of cleavages.

'By what?' Carly challenged, frowning.

'By your sang-froid,' Lorenzo said easily with a smile. 'Why, Carly, you're shivering,' he said as she shuddered with awareness. 'Are you cold?'

All the tiny hairs on the back of her neck were standing to attention, and her nipples were about to explode, but cold? No, she wasn't cold.

'It's time you made your way to your table. I trust you won't let me down?'

'I won't let myself down,' she assured him pleasantly. 'What are you doing?' she said with suspicion as he uncapped his pen.

'Not taking any chances,' he murmured.

'Meaning?'

'I'm changing our names around on the seating plan so I can watch your back…'

She was tempted to relent and think that, for once, Lorenzo was trying to be nice, when just at that moment Madeline Du Pre wafted past with a coterie of admirers. The sight of her main rival for the scholarship flagging up her good sense in front of Lorenzo was all it took for Carly to decide to stay and fight in her orange armour. Removing the pen from Lorenzo's fingers, she changed their names back again, scratching his alterations out with such force she bent his nib.

There had been catcalls and wolf-whistles all night as pupils rose one by one to make their application to join the circuit. Silence fell when Carly stood. Maybe everyone was bored of the sport; her name was pretty close to the end of the alphabet. Or perhaps the seniors had simply exhausted their catalogue of jibes. Or, and this seemed the most likely explanation, the orange gown had come into its own and stunned everyone into silence.

'My name is Carly Viola Tate, and I was called to the bar by the honourable society of…'

It took the space of a heartbeat for her mind to blank. Her lips tried to form the words she needed to speak while her mind was in freefall. *Which of the ancient Inns of Court had she been called to the bar by?* Her darting gaze met Lorenzo's. She only had to take one look at that lazy, mocking stare to know she had no intention of allowing him to see her fail. He must have been through a similar ordeal at some stage of his career…

As had all the seniors here before her!

Tipping her chin, she started over.

The seniors would have to look elsewhere for their sport. Lorenzo didn't know when he had felt so relieved…or more aroused. And that did stop him in his tracks. But as he basked in the compliments of his peers over the outstanding performance of his pupil he could only agree with them that Carly was indeed exceptional—and in so many ways. She had obliterated his addiction to all that was perfect, replacing it with new standards of her own. She was quirky and different and fresh. Or, to put it another way, her breasts were extraordinarily large and she was divinely plump in all the right places…though he had to admit that her fashion sense still left everything to be desired.

But, of course, he had to forget this moment of weakness and remember their relative positions in life. He was dominant, while she was…

No.

No!

She was not spread-eagled on his bed!

She was his *young* student, and the development of her career devolved on him. She was inexperienced and innocent, and it was up to him to defend her. And didn't he excel in defending the innocent?

He curbed his smile, confining himself to a grave nod of approval as she glanced at him in triumph before sitting down to a chorus of cheers and wolf-whistles. She had been so charming, so endearing when she stumbled over her little speech, everyone had loved her for it. Even the seniors had forgotten to heckle, and the dreadful gown had been overlooked. As her pupil master, restraint was the only sensible option to him, but unfortunately that had no effect on his libido. Lucky for him he was about to be removed from temptation. The courts were about to close for the Christmas recess and when they did he would work off his excess energy on the ski slopes.

With his conscience set at ease, Lorenzo turned his attention to the man seated next to him, and was soon involved in the sort of work-based discussion lawyers thrived on. But try as he might he couldn't keep his thoughts from wandering back to Carly. He wanted her so badly his balls ached.

CHAPTER FOUR

SHE HAD RETURNED HOME in triumph to this? Cramming a pillow over her head, Carly tried not to hear the noises coming from the next room. Her flatmate appeared to be indulging in some sort of technically advanced sex moves, which required the bed to bang against the wall in one rhythm while Louisa cried out in another. The result was a complex syncopation of which Stravinsky would have been proud.

Didn't anyone sleep these days?

Was everyone in London, except for her, having sex?

Swinging out of bed, Carly squinted at the clock and saw that it was one o'clock in the morning. Great. Shuffling out of the room in her dinosaur-claw slippers, she fumbled for the light switch and turned it on.

'Hello, Carly…'

'Lorenzo! What on earth are you doing here?'

'Nice to see you too…' Sliding the silk scarf off his neck, he looked her up and down, bestowing sensation upon each one of her erogenous zones in turn.

Her cheeks fired automatically. Knuckling her eyes she tried to convince herself that this could only be a very bad dream.

'Well?' he said when she stood in his way. 'Aren't you going to invite me in?'

'You *are* in,' she pointed out.

Shrugging off his coat, Lorenzo handed it to her with the scarf. She was wearing a paper-thin nightshirt that covered nothing. Tugging hard on the hem in an attempt to cover her bottom, she exposed a breast.

Lorenzo watched without comment, and then his gaze tracked down to study her dinosaur-claw slippers.

Turning on her heel, she hung up his coat. What was she doing *waiting on him?* She could only excuse herself by pleading the lateness of the hour and her exhaustion after the ordeal of the Grand Court.

He had telephoned every hotel in London when his new flat flooded. Not a chance of a bed in town with Christmas looming, he'd been told. He had tried absolutely every option until bunking down in the spare room of a flat owned by an old school chum became the only option. The repairs to his own apartment would be completed within the next couple of days, but until then, this was it...

As Carly stared at him in disbelief, he asked himself if a park bench have been a better option? Did he want to take up residence with his pupil? Did he want to have temptation thrust in his face? Did he want to smell her warm, fresh, sleepy smell and see her hair in wild disarray? Her face was attractively sleep crumpled and she was half-naked...

'What are you doing here, Lorenzo?' she challenged him.

He was guilty of musing while Carly's mental faculties had stormed back onto full alert. 'I might ask you the same question,' he returned smoothly.

'Louisa is my friend, and this is her apartment,' she told him, coughing noisily to cover the sounds of passion erupting from a bedroom down the hall.

'And Louisa's brother is my friend,' he explained. 'They

share joint tenancy on the flat. So while some emergency repairs are being carried out on my new apartment I'll be using the spare room here—'

'You can't,' she exploded. 'I live here.'

'And for the time being, I do too,' he informed her. 'Is the coffee on?' He strolled down the hall following the odour of old pizza and tea bags.

What did Lorenzo imagine this was? Carly raged silently. *A service flat?* Counting to ten, she took the opportunity to rattle her brain cells into some sort of order.

'Do you have anything better than instant coffee?' he called from the kitchen.

She found him rooting around and peering into cupboards. 'There might be some beans in there, somewhere…' There might be lions too, for all she knew.

'Along with the spaghetti hoops, Pop Tarts and… What are these?' He held up a tub and pulled a face. 'Pot Noodles?' He narrowed his eyes in disapproval as he looked down at her.

She responded in the usual way to Lorenzo in stern mood, and, after enjoying it for a moment or two, told him, 'I haven't had time to go shopping recently. I've been very busy at work.'

'Really?' he said, as if this came as a complete surprise to him. 'Well, you still have to eat.' He looked her up and down. 'We wouldn't want you shrinking away…'

We wouldn't? Clearing her throat to muffle another of Louisa's moans, she became obsessed by turning all the labels on the tins to the front.

'You must keep up your strength,' Lorenzo advised, reaching past her into the darkest part of the cupboard.

For the battles to come, she could only presume. 'You mean I should arm myself for disappointment?'

When Lorenzo turned to look at her his arm was still outstretched and very close to her face…so close it made her cheeks tingle.

'Disappointment?' he queried.

She watched his lips work in fascination.

'Why do you say that? You did well tonight. I'm proud of you…'

Lorenzo was proud of her? For a moment she just stared and inhaled his cologne—sandalwood and amber, with a hint of wild fig and cassis. And still her analytical mind refused to shut down. What was Lorenzo really up to? Why was he here? Was he serious when he said they were going to be living together? Even in the short-term that would be more fuel for her fantasies than she could safely handle.

Living together?

It was time for a dash of cold reality in the face. This was not a dream come true; this was her worst nightmare. Where would she take refuge from Lorenzo's scorn now? She would be on duty every minute of the day and night. 'How long did you say you would be staying?'

'I didn't.' He turned back to his search.

'Weeks?'

'*Dio!* No!'

He sounded about as excited by that prospect as she felt. 'Oh, well, that's a relief.'

'Because my being here is your worst nightmare, I presume?' He turned slowly to look at her, erasing all sensible thought from her mind. 'Don't look so worried,' he murmured, turning back to his search. ' I'll only be staying here until they repair the pipes and restore all the damage done to my apartment.'

His apartment… Images of leopard skin rugs dressed with naked women sprang unbidden into Carly's mind. All the women would be slim and beautiful, of course. How long would that take to organise?

Unfortunately, she didn't get a chance to progress this thought as a series of shrieks erupted from Louisa's bedroom.

'Where is Louisa, by the way?' Lorenzo said, frowning as the shrieks continued unabated.

'Asleep in bed,' Carly said hurriedly. 'She must be having a nightmare.'

'It sounds like a good one to me,' Lorenzo murmured. Taking a step towards the kitchen door, he turned. 'Do you think she's all right, or should I intervene?'

'I'm sure she's fine.' Carly wasn't sure whether to be more horrified by the screams or by her restraining hand on Lorenzo's arm. She removed it smartly before telling him, 'I think we'd better leave her to sleep now, don't you?'

'All right,' he agreed, clearly enjoying every moment of her discomfort.

'Why don't you and I have a drink?' she suggested, keen to keep Lorenzo occupied in the kitchen until things calmed down a bit along the hall. 'Coffee, water, or something stronger…?'

'In the absence of decent coffee, water, please,' he said.

She added ice to the glass of water before handing it to him.

Lounging back against the counter-top, he tipped his glass towards her in an ironic salute. 'Goodnight, Carly…'

Yes, why exactly was she hanging around?

'I wouldn't advise you to be late for my class twice in one week…'

He let out a breath of relief as the kitchen door shut behind her. Five minutes in Carly's company had left him in torment, real physical pain. This was the craziest situation, and he only had himself to blame. Had he really thought it would be easy to be under the same roof as Carly just because his palate was so jaded?

Jaded?

Not tonight!

She was different and he wanted her. It was that simple and that complicated. This was torture. He'd be close to her night and day and couldn't touch. He'd award himself a medal when this was over.

Tossing and turning on her bed, Carly tried telling herself what a relief it was Lorenzo didn't want her 'that way'. But as Louisa's sexual marathon continued she knew she didn't want to be a dumpling with freckles; she wanted to be a fully formed sex kitten with the power to bring Lorenzo to his knees. But Lorenzo was glamorous and rich, while she was not. He was at the top of the greasy career pole, while she was at the bottom—and would never climb any higher if she went on like this.

Stifling the alarm clock with a well-aimed pillow, Carly concluded that the only way to impress Lorenzo was in the professional arena. She would win the scholarship, and she would arrange the best Christmas party in the history of Christmas parties. How, she hadn't a clue, but that was a minor detail right now. Stumbling out of bed, she blundered blindly into the hallway where fortunately Lorenzo was there to catch her when she fell over a shoe.

'Don't be late,' he said, steadying her back on her feet.

Was she imagining it, or had he snatched his hands off her body as he might from a live electric cable? She'd got quite a charge herself, but in her case she wouldn't have minded waiting around until her hair sizzled.

For the sake of her career she decided prudence must be her watchword. 'Good morning, Lorenzo. I trust you slept well?'

He made a humming sound as he looked her up and down, reminding her to hide her fat rolls beneath a robe in future. As the door slammed behind him she found herself waiting for a thunderclap, but of course there was only silence and a great big empty hole. Lorenzo didn't so much as glance behind him; any erotic thoughts floating about were confined to her own head.

Deflated, Carly trundled towards the kitchen, where a double-sized bowl of honey-sweet-quadruple-the-calories pops awaited her.

Flat share with Lorenzo was shaping up to be about as appealing as eating her way through a case of stewed prunes. Shelving the scholarship plan suddenly seemed like a very good idea, but nothing would disappoint her parents more. They had sacrificed everything for her, and she owed them this last and most prestigious scholarship, which in turn meant she couldn't afford to fall foul of Lorenzo because her pupilage hung by a thread he could cut.

Pupilage, the system whereby a practising barrister monitored the training of a graduate law student, was like gold dust. If you lost your pupilage for any reason your career at the bar was as good as over. Failure wasn't an option, especially not to a Tate. The law had bypassed a generation in the family, and Carly had always known her destiny as the plain sister. She had to uphold the family tradition. Some grizzled ancestor had probably dipped a nib in their own blood to sign the Magna Carta.

At least she wasn't late for her appointment with Lorenzo. Knocking on his door and entering the room, she found him lounging back in his chair.

'Progress report, Christmas party,' he instructed with a wave of his hand like some maestro bringing in the soloist.

Carly's mind blanked as she looked at his socks. They were pink today. And not just pink—fuchsia-pink!

Did it matter if his socks were pink? This was a man who

could wear a dress and look virile, which he almost did in court, come to think of it, in his wig and gown—

'Ms Tate, are you still with me?'

The voice was impatient.

'The list?'

The hand signal unmistakable.

'Of course.' Tilting her chin at a businesslike angle, she offered him the sheet of paper listing everything she had prepared. 'It doesn't include all the details yet.'

'I don't like guessing games.'

'And this won't be one.' She sincerely hoped.

Scanning the page, he made no comment. He was beginning to make her feel nervous. Why was life so unjust? Why did Lorenzo look as if he was ready for a photo shoot for the world's most desirable man, while she felt as usual like the dumpling on parade? She forced herself to meet the icy gaze unflinching as he glanced up.

'Not bad, but it would be better if you work to a theme.'

Praise indeed! What a shame she wasn't ready to reveal that in fact she *was* working to a theme, if not the sort of theme she guessed Lorenzo would be expecting.

'What I need now,' he said, 'are specifics. Detail, Ms Tate.'

Resisting the urge to salute, she stared past him out through the panoramic windows overlooking the city. Somewhere out there were all the answers to her problems. At least, those connected to the party. 'I need a little more time. You'll just have to trust me.'

'Trust you?' One ebony brow shot up, showing Lorenzo's opinion of that suggestion. 'I thought I'd explained to you that the only thing I'm interested in is fact?'

But this wasn't a court case, and she wasn't on trial. She held her ground, staring straight into his incredible eyes. 'I don't want to spoil the surprise.' This was a phrase she had often heard trip off her mother's tongue. It was only as she grew to be older that she realised her mother employed it to cover a bottomless pit of panic.

Lorenzo wasn't even slightly fooled. 'Arranging the Christmas party isn't a leisure activity, Ms Tate; it's part of your brief as my junior. It's also an opportunity to show everyone what you're capable of.'

Exactly, Carly thought uncomfortably.

'I want a detailed summary of everything you've arranged up to now. Come,' he said, offering her a pen, 'write them down for me now.' Ripping a clean sheet of paper from his pad, he handed it to her and sat back.

It was a very large sheet of paper for what was destined to be a very short list. 'Why don't I take it with me so I don't disturb you?'

'Sit down,' he rapped.

They stared at each other unblinking for a moment, but then an image of her parents' anxious faces swam into Carly's mind and she folded. 'Okay...'

'And while you're writing your list I'd like you to start thinking about guidelines for some of the younger members of chambers. There will be a number of senior judges attending this year, some of whom wear ermine and sit in the House of Lords. I don't expect anyone here to let the side down.'

He watched her face carefully. Sometimes he surprised himself with the ingenuity of his tests. This one was particularly harsh, because it put her in the firing line in front of her colleagues. Could she rise above that and act professionally? Could she swallow her misgivings? Or was this the moment when she told him to go to hell and walked out? He decided to find out.

'You will need two lists,' he told her as if she were in infant class. 'One will have the heading "Christmas Party", and the second will have the heading "Christmas Party Guidelines for Junior Members of Chambers".'

That should win her a few friends! Was there a way out? If there was she couldn't think of one. For now she would have to be satisfied with some fiendish revenge sequences reeling through her mind involving Lorenzo naked and a pair of stiletto heels. But later, when she got back to her cubby-hole, she would have to work something out that didn't risk the scholarship, or her easy working relationship with her younger colleagues...

'What?' Lorenzo said, glancing up.

Had he felt the sparks flying his way? Carly wondered, composing her face into its customary bland mask. Composing a cautionary note for her fellow pupils as Lorenzo had in-structed was nothing short of an insult to them, and to her...

'What is it, Ms Tate?'

'Nothing,' she said innocently, but an idea was forming; an idea that involved two lists for Lorenzo as he had re-quested, and a third, somewhat less reverential, list for her friends.

'Well, if that's all?' Lorenzo said, turning back to his notes. 'Get on with it.'

He was right. There was no point in prolonging this. She was a realist, if nothing else, and as Lorenzo was all male, while she was undeniably female, there was no common ground.

'Write,' he insisted, staring hard at her sheet of paper.

She tried. She sucked the tip of her pen and tried really hard. She had the ideas—too many of them! The problem was assembling them in front of him. Lorenzo made it so hard to concentrate. She was drowning in waves of testosterone, and then there was his distinctive scent, warm, clean, male and spicy. She could close her eyes and inhale that all day quite happily… Except at the same time she would have to wriggle now and then to give the type of sensations he provoked chance to express themselves. Come to think of it, she hadn't been so obsessed by sex for years—not since she had lost her virginity to a spotty youth on the back seat of his car; a skirmish that had hardly prepared her for encountering Lorenzo. She'd had no idea she had been so repressed—

'Okay, leave now and take your work with you,' he snapped impatiently. 'I can see you're not concentrating, and you're distracting me.'

He watched her leap away as if she were attached to a spring. Was he such an ogre? Or had that wriggle signalled more than a desire to get away? 'Before you go…'

'Yes?'

Her face had reddened guiltily. What had she been dreaming about—his demise, perhaps?

Okay, so maybe he was being hard on her, but he expected the best of his students, and Carly was the best of the best. Organising the Christmas party was a thankless task; the list of guidelines he had proposed she draw up a mockery. He could imagine the reaction of her colleagues to any suggestions she might make! But lawyers had to keep a cool head under fire. Would she? He decided to push a little harder and find out. 'I'm meeting a friend tonight.'

A muscle jumped in her jaw though her face remained carefully expressionless. This ability to hide her thoughts was yet one more reason she currently headed up the list of potential Unicorn scholarship candidates. 'I'm going to bring my guest back to the flat, and I thought you might like to make yourself useful…'

If her face grew any tighter she would implode. He pressed on. 'Make sure the wine is chilled, prepare a few canapés, that sort of thing?'

He could see her feminist principles raging against her lust to win the scholarship. He could also see her wanting to take him by the throat and choke him. And throughout all this they continued to stare at each other impassively.

Easing her neck, Carly fought to stay calm. 'Canapés?' She could only comfort herself with the thought that the reports of her numerous culinary disasters hadn't reached Lorenzo's ears yet.

The successful candidate for the Unicorn scholarship will be both resourceful and creative…

'Of course, no problem,' she replied.

'That's good,' he said, relaxing. 'You might want to sit in when my guest arrives as we'll be discussing the possibility of extending the reach of the scholarship. It's such a great opportunity.'

To make canapés? Carly thought, staring back without expression.

'As I'm sure you'll agree?' Lorenzo challenged, searching her gaze for the slightest hint of insubordination. 'Canapés at eight, then?'

Why not? She had no intention of being tripped up by a cocktail sausage now.

CHAPTER FIVE

CARLY GAZED AT the work she had completed with satisfaction. It felt good to be properly organised, almost like the old times before Lorenzo had exploded onto the scene. She had compiled three lists, two of which, being dry and sensible, were the ones for Lorenzo.

The Christmas Party list would show him how bookings for various services were working out as well as the ordering system she was using—everything except food was either on a short-term hire agreement, or a sale and return basis, so he could find no room for concern there. The Christmas Party Guidelines for her colleagues would appear equally sensible—because, of course, Lorenzo wouldn't be seeing the copy she'd actually send to her colleagues, or, indeed, her own copy, upon which she had added some rather graphic doodles.

In addition to this she had stuck a Post-It note to the desk on which she had scrawled, 'Canapés at eight!' To date she had made no entries to suggest what form these canapés might take. But there was plenty of time to worry about that. Canapés were tiny, which suggested they were easy to prepare. It was more important to concentrate on her doodles, which in Carly's modest opinion were starting to rival the illustrations in the Kama Sutra. Well, a girl could dream, couldn't she? And with Lorenzo tied up in court she had hours in which to indulge every flight of erotic fancy she'd ever had…

By noon Carly's Christmas Party list had a pleasing line of ticks down the side of the page. Father Christmas had been booked, along with a couple of elves, and even on such a slim budget she had managed to organise good, wholesome food, that could best be described as interesting. Or, at least, she hoped it would prove so to the sophisticated palate of those attending. Anyway, she liked it, and it was in line with the theme she had chosen, so Lorenzo could hardly complain.

When it came to the advisory notes for her colleagues she had thought long and hard before deciding on something they could stomach. She knew Lorenzo had set her up for a fall and she had every intention of staying upright.

With this intention in mind she kept the tone light, listing the warnings beneath a picture of Lorenzo looking suitably stern and yet rather stunning in his wig and gown. Her fellow pupils would get the joke. Especially after she'd added some doodles to their list—the one Lorenzo wouldn't be seeing—the list she would compile after this one to illustrate the form any rebellion might take. But meanwhile Lorenzo's list was complete:

GUIDELINES CHRISTMAS PARTY
REMEMBER…
MERRY NIGHTS MAKE SAD MORNINGS!
And here are a few handy tips to help *you* avoid the pitfalls…
1. Arrive early and make a point of speaking to your immediate superior!
2. Above all, please remember that first impressions count!

3. You must remain visible at all times and maintain a pleasant and interested smile on your face.

4. You must try to engage every judge in light-hearted chit-chat, and maintain an air of quiet confidence as you do so.

5. Absolutely NO dancing drunkenly on tables!

6. In the unlikely event that you begin to feel the effects of too much alcohol you must take yourself outside the building IMMEDIATELY!

7. The importance of thanking your host at the end of the night cannot be overstated.

Lorenzo should be pleased with that. Folding the sheet of paper neatly, she placed it safely inside an envelope.

And now for the list her colleagues would receive, which would be basically the same, but with certain additions. Her intention was to make it recognisably the same, so they wouldn't be caught out if questioned, and yet, so very, *very* different…

Beneath the legend *'GUIDELINES CHRISTMAS PARTY'* the banner heading still read 'MERRY NIGHTS MAKE SAD MORNINGS!' But now there was a smaller sub-heading, which advised,

Expert Schmoozing, Without Resorting To Being A Creep, Helps You Move *UP* The Ladder!

Below this she had written another list of bullet points.

Arrive early and make a point of speaking to your immediate superior!

Carly frowned, reading the point through again. The chance of engaging Lorenzo in a conversation that didn't involve her saluting and him instructing seemed remote. And weren't parties supposed to be fun? She added fangs and horns to his picture before printing out a dozen for distribution.

The importance of thanking the host cannot be overstated.

She frowned again. Well, that was all very well, but Lorenzo hadn't made it clear who would be hosting the party. She added a handwritten note to suggest her colleagues assume the customary grovelling position with every senior who attended.

You must remain visible at all times and maintain a pleasant and interested smile on your face.

No problem! Smiling while inwardly yawning was a skill every pupil perfected within their first six months. But she added a further helpful point anyway:

You must try to engage even the most curmudgeonly judge in light-hearted chit-chat, and maintain an air of quiet confidence as you do so...

Even if they fell asleep on the bench last time you were in front of them, presumably.

Absolutely NO dancing drunkenly on tables!

After a moment's contemplation she moved this item to the top of the list and reprinted everything, shredding the first draft and anything else that might prove incriminating. Then she popped the lists into envelopes ready for distribution. It was crucial to ensure they didn't get into the wrong hands—i.e. Lorenzo's hands. To make certain of it she would deliver them to the various offices herself.

Sitting back, Carly congratulated herself on a job well done, and then, remembering that there was still time to personalise her own set of guidelines, she got started…

First off she jotted a note next to Lorenzo's photograph: 'Carly's Christmas Present to Herself', while down the side of the page she sketched some imaginative and energetic matchstick people—one of whom wore Technicolor socks, while the other boasted enormous breasts…

He had just walked back into chambers when Carly rushed past him with a distracted look on her face. She was muttering something. He thought she said, 'Canapés…'

As she ran out of the door a note fluttered out of her pocket. Strictly speaking he shouldn't read someone else's mail, but lawyers did it all the time…

Returning to his office, he drew out the note and scanned it. It was a list Carly had headed, *'GUIDELINES CHRIST-MAS PARTY'*. So far so good, but then he realised that this list bore scant resemblance to the one she had put in his pigeon-hole. His gaze returned to study the various doodles she had drawn down the side of it. Her inventions were impressive. He read on: 'Inappropriate behaviour at the Christmas party can SERIOUSLY limit your career…'

How fortunate for him that rules were made to be broken, and when you reached the inner circle you broke them all the time.

Canapés!

Carly woke up with a start. For a moment she couldn't remember where she was. Where she had been was far preferable…in Lorenzo's arms, and he had been just about to kiss her. She rubbed the back of her hand across her mouth just to check she hadn't been playing Sleeping Beauty and missed something wonderful.

Not a chance! It was so hot in her little cubby-hole she had fallen asleep, that was all. And no wonder she was exhausted after her shopping expedition. Propelled into panic by the sight of Lorenzo in Reception, she had rushed to the supermarket, but halfway there she had spotted a sign advertising a sale of designer shoes...

Glancing at her wrist-watch, she let out a shriek.

All thoughts of Lorenzo and stiletto heels flew from her mind. Flailing about, she battled to organise her wayward thoughts and only succeeded in knocking everything off her desk, then banging her head against it when she dived to retrieve it. Nursing the bump she ordered her inner self to calm down. Canapés were no problem. They'd been in her head all the time she'd been asleep, so the planning was already done. All she had to do now was buy the ingredients and assemble them. The menu she had decided upon was divine... Shrimp in a light batter with sweet chilli sauce; slivers of tomato on tiny rye crackers with an anchovy curled artistically on top and—the pièce de résistance—miniature parcels of smoked salmon and cream cheese decorated with chopped chives.

Inwardly, she dribbled.

'You're in a hurry today...'

Lorenzo's lazy drawl caught her between the shoulder blades and brought her screaming to a halt. She turned to look at him and felt her senses flare like the bright socks he was wearing—purple with orange flags today. She made a silent vow to carry out intensive research on international marine signals the moment she got the chance.

'Canapés all in hand?' he said, giving her a dark stare.

Her throat dried. 'In component form…'

'Excellent…'

There was something different about Lorenzo; she couldn't quite pin it down. Maybe it was the way he was looking at her. Normally he made inscrutable seem an understatement; he wasn't a top lawyer for nothing. But today there was a definite smoulder in his gaze as he leaned back against the wall.

So, who was he thinking about?

The sting of jealousy that brought on took Carly by surprise. She ran a mental check-list of all her female colleagues, wondering which one of them had served Lorenzo's best interest that lunchtime, and knew she didn't stand a chance of making that list. Lorenzo probably thought plain girls didn't need sex like pretty women, but that didn't stop her wanting him. Especially now when he looked so gorgeous…absolutely gorgeous—

'No time to hang around,' he cautioned, stamping on her fantasy.

It was a waste of time dreaming, Carly thought, heading for the door. Lorenzo was on another planet, one where men ruled and women served—mostly in the bedroom when they weren't trying to fold towels a certain way, or create the world's most impressive canapé…

She took one last look at him before the door swung shut and decided he looked pretty pleased with himself. No wonder! The clerks probably kept his little black book alongside Lorenzo's court appointment diary to enable him to take full advantage of each adjournment. Plus he'd just gained a slave of cuisine. Who wouldn't be feeling smug?

So, how did she explain why the heart of this independent-minded woman was racing with delight at the thought of serving him?

Because like a cup of hot chocolate thick enough to stand a spoon in, Lorenzo Domenico was wicked, but irresistible.

Carly's hope of presenting the perfect canapé faltered at the entrance of the twenty-four-hour supermarket. She stood outside staring through the plate-glass window at people fighting over Christmas food and just knew she couldn't face it. Turning on her heel, she hurried across the street towards Greasy Jo's. The local pizza parlour had never let her down…

By half past seven she was back at the flat carving up pizza in the kitchen. She heard the front door open and Lorenzo and his friend come in.

Lorenzo and male friend…

Thank goodness! She wasn't sure that even for the sake of the scholarship she could have waited on some It girl with the hots for Lorenzo!

Giving her hands a final lick, she wiped them down the front of her jeans, and then, picking up the platter of oozing pizza, she backed her way into the sitting room and turned around with a flourish. 'Gentlemen…'

Two pieces of pizza flew off the plate.

She ignored the startled glances and carried on. Dipping low, she offered, 'Gorgonzola and gherkin, pickled onion and pastrami, or…' and she was rather proud of this one '…squid ink and pineapple…'

Beneath his tan Lorenzo paled. 'Thank you, Carly. Perhaps you'd like to put them down over there?' He indicated the furthest corner of the room. 'And then perhaps you'd like to pour the chilled white wine?' He said this in a slightly harder voice.

The *chilled* white wine?

'Of course…' She gave a little laugh, scooping up the pizza on the floor as she made her escape.

* * *

Exchanging an amused shrug with his friend as he went to retrieve the plate, Lorenzo said, 'Excuse my pupil. She's embarked on a rather steep learning curve—'

'Drawn up by you?' Ronan's lips pressed down. 'Pass the pizza, will you? I'm starving.'

'Me too,' Lorenzo confessed. He and Ronan had been students together; they'd eat anything. Not that Carly needed to know that! 'So, what d'you think of her?'

'You're a lucky man. She's gorgeous.'

'Do you think so?' He played it cool.

Ronan gave him a look. 'How long do you intend to keep up the tough-tutor act?'

'For as long as it takes.'

Ronan raised his yet-to-be-filled glass in a toast to him, while he called unrepentantly, 'Carly—wine.'

'Lorenzo…' Ronan remonstrated, shaking his head in disapproval.

But he knew he'd be lucky if he didn't get that wine poured over his head, Lorenzo thought, already smiling as he anticipated the banter that would ensue between him and Carly once Ronan left.

Carly ignored Lorenzo's summons. Leaning against the kitchen door, she thought back to when she had been such a together sort of person—that was before Lorenzo came along, of course. Now she barely knew her own name, let alone remembered to chill the wine. There was only one thing for it…

Rinsing off some ice cubes from the back of the box, she dropped them into the wineglasses, filled them to the brim with warm white wine and stirred vigorously.

Lorenzo's stare found her face like a heat-seeking missile

the moment she came back into the room. Lifting the wine-glass, he held it up to the light without comment.

'So you liked the pizza?' she said with relief, glad something had gone well. She handed Ronan a glass of wine.

'We had to throw it down,' Lorenzo said solemnly, staring out of the window.

'Into the dumper?' Carly exclaimed, glancing in the same direction and then at the empty plate. But even as she gasped she was sure she saw Lorenzo exchange one of his wicked grins with Ronan. As she stood there the two men clinked their glasses, and with gusto the ice cubes collided.

'Ice?' Lorenzo's stare didn't so much burn into her as presage Armageddon.

Ronan tried to soften the situation, suggesting pleasantly, 'Aren't you going to join us, Carly?'

He turned to look at his friend as a stab of something unaccustomed took him by surprise. It wasn't jealousy, of course, more head-of-the-herd instinct. Well, Ronan was no angel, and it was up to him to defend his pupil. 'My apologies, Carly,' he said sternly. 'Allow me to present Ronan O'Connor, a friend of mine and a trader in futures. Ronan, this is my pupil, Carly Tate…'

Ronan gave Carly a sympathetic look as he stood to shake her hand.

'We're discussing the possibility of extending the Unicorn scholarship to the City,' Lorenzo explained to Carly. 'Would you care to join us?'

Sit between them while they drank Lorenzo's expensive wine, which she had watered down with ice cubes? No, thank you! It was time to head for the badlands away from Lorenzo's accusing stare!

She didn't want to brood in her bedroom either, Carly

realised, not with Lorenzo in her head darkly mocking. She was going to dress up, go out, and show him!

After making a somewhat feeble excuse about leaving the men to it, she went to her room to get ready. Faded jeans wouldn't cut it, and so she ditched them in favour of a black spangled top from a charity shop, along with a short denim skirt from the same place. And then, because she'd always known they'd come in useful, she unpacked the killer heels she'd bought at the sale.

Lorenzo would never guess it was all a sham. The tip tap of heels on a laminate floor would tell him everything she wanted him to know. She was a sophisticated city girl in full control of her life.

CHAPTER SIX

THE BAR CARLY was heading for was popular with young city types, and tonight it seemed busier than ever. Odd for mid-week, but perhaps not when you considered that this was the lead up to Christmas…

Peering in through the tinted windows, she felt daunted. She had only been for a drink in a crowd before. She tried to identify a free table before taking the plunge, but then a few spots of rain hit her in the face, forcing her to act.

Noise and warmth hit her as she walked inside. An earnest young man in designer jeans and a smart black top came towards her right away. 'Ah, good,' he said, as if he had been expecting her. 'You're just in time.' Without any explanation he grabbed her elbow and started steering her through the throng. She was about to protest he'd got the wrong person, but then she noticed he was leading her towards an empty table. At least she'd get the chance to sit down and read her book. Buzzy? The place was heaving.

At least this wasn't Lorenzo's type of place, Carly con-soled herself, pulling out her novel. But as she tried to read Lorenzo's face replaced the cover, the first page, the second, and the— Slamming the book shut, she tried to attract a waiter. This was an emergency! What she needed was coffee: hot, sweet and strong.

* * *

Lorenzo made coffee and then settled down with Ronan to chat about old times, but he kept thinking about Carly and an image of her alone and unprotected in the city sharpened in his mind.

He'd caught sight of her as she click-clacked past the door, and she'd been dressed up by Carly's standards. Surely he'd have heard on the chambers grapevine if there'd been a party, which left a meeting in a bar or in a restaurant. It had to be close by because she hadn't called a taxi, and the nearest tube or bus stop was over a mile away. She had definitely planned to walk, but not far in those heels…

It was pitch-black outside and the rain was turning to sleet. He couldn't kid himself any longer; he'd been hard on her and that was why she'd gone out. What was more important to him? Carly's safety and happiness, or an evening chatting with his pal?

'Oh, no, thank you, I brought a book with me…'

'But not this book,' the young woman said confidently, plonking one from the pile in her arms down in front of Carly before disappearing back into the crowd.

She tried to attract the attention of an attendant to hand the glossy booklet back. She was here to relax, not to be drawn into something that put such a flush on people's faces.

Having failed, she found as she had suspected that it wasn't so much a book as a marketing tool, entitled, *Raise Your Market Value,* but it was the subheading that caught her attention: 'Make contact, make chat, make love…' She jerked around to take a closer look at everyone else in the bar.

'Is this chair free?'

She panicked and stood up.

'Please don't go,' the man said plaintively. 'I'm desperate to make contact with something other than a cyber chip—'

Knocked back into her seat by a fresh rush of people she

made a silent pledge to give it five minutes and then she was out of here.

'Is this your first time?' the man asked her.

And the last, Carly decided, noticing he seemed fixated by her breasts.

'We've made a good start, haven't we?' he said.

Had they? Had they made a good start? If so she was giving out the wrong signals! Glancing round, she dreaded Lorenzo walking in, and yet wished he would.

Then just as a bell sounded a man stepped out of the rain. The collar of his rugged jacket was pulled up tight, revealing a hint of the casual chequered shirt underneath. Snug-fitting blue jeans teamed with workman-like boots added to the piratical image created by the rough, dark stubble on his face. His unruly black hair curled damply round his chiselled cheekbones, and his eyes were narrowed as he searched the room.

Lorenzo!

Waitresses swarmed round him, and then looked her way.

Escape! was the only thought in her head, but the bell had been a signal for everyone to move, or so it seemed. She was jostled and staggered as she tottered determinedly towards the nearest door. The handle seemed so temptingly close, yet as she launched herself forward to grab it the man who had been at her table got in the way.

'No,' he said, shaking his arm free as she clutched hold of him to steady herself. 'Only we men move around. You women have to stay at your table.'

'I'm sorry?'

'You've had your five minutes with me,' he explained self-importantly. 'If I tick your box at the end of the evening you might get five minutes more.'

Tick her box? Urgh! That sounded horrible! But the

thought of Lorenzo delivering one of his fire-and-thunder sermons was even worse—

Deciding the man was the best shield she'd got, Carly hid behind him, but he made some rude comment, which prompted everyone to turn to look at them. And now Lorenzo was staring too!

'Ah, there you are,' Lorenzo said with satisfaction. 'What's this about?' His dark gaze switched to the face of the other man, forcing a nervous laugh from him.

'Perhaps you should ask your young lady—'

'Perhaps I will,' Lorenzo said icily. 'Intending to take advantage of her, were you?' he suggested.

'Not at all! She came on to me—'

'To you?' Lorenzo's raised brow was enough for some of his audience to start laughing.

'Yes. I think she was trying to kiss me!' *Shock! Horror!* 'She doesn't seem to appreciate the finer points of speed dating. The regulations demand—'

Speed dating? What a clutz! Carly felt as if someone had sewn a running thread through her stomach and pulled it tight.

'To which regulations are you referring?' Lorenzo demanded in his deceptively mild court tone, commanding everyone's attention.

'We get given five minutes with each woman, and then I tick her box if I'm interested. I haven't made up my mind yet,' the man declared with affront.

'I think you have,' Lorenzo told him. 'Did you come on to this man?' he demanded, switching his attention to Carly. 'Did you want him to kiss you?'

'Of course not!' she protested hotly in possibly the most humiliating moment of her whole life.

'Then why did you come here?' the man cut in.

'If you want a kiss so badly, I'll kiss you,' Lorenzo offered.

Was there anyone else in the world who could *accidentally* speed date? He thought not. And it only made Carly all the more adorable in his eyes. How alone she must have felt to come here in the first place. And whose fault was that? Time to make amends.

Carly gulped as Lorenzo dragged her into his arms. What happened next was less a kiss, and more a lifetime achievement award in seduction, and it went on and on until people started applauding. First he laced his fingers through her hair, while with his other hand he caressed her cheeks. He made her feel as if she were the most beautiful woman in the world, stroking her jaw with his thumb as he kissed her, and kissing her so tenderly she could hardly believe this was what people did. And then the kiss morphed into something so stirring and passionate, she had to wonder if he'd forgotten himself as he plunged and withdrew in what was surely a dress rehearsal for a performance she had no part in.

Drawing back at last, he stared deep into her eyes, and then, taking her by surprise, he came back for more. This couldn't be a mistake, could it? She hoped not. Lorenzo's face was still cold from the night air, and his stubble felt rough against her cheek, but his lips were hot with a persuasive heat that ran riot through her body and as he continued to kiss her their audience egged them on.

'I think I'd better get you out of here,' he said, pulling away at last.

He was still holding on to her. 'I think you better had,' Carly agreed, her eyes sparkling like diamonds.

CHAPTER SEVEN

HE WAS TAKING CARLY out of the bar when a girl approached him with a clipboard, to ask if, under the happy circumstance, he would be prepared to give her company an endorsement. She might have spared a thought for Carly's opinion on that, he thought, but the young woman's gaze was fixed on him.

'I don't sign my name to anything unless I've read the small print,' he told her, concentrating on ushering Carly safely towards the door. He took the pamphlet anyway and stuffed it in his pocket. 'I'll study this later, and find out what exactly your company is asking people to sign up to.'

The girl looked as if she wanted it back. He didn't blame her.

Carly noted the incident, but was still reeling from what had happened. With Lorenzo's arm around her shoulders it was hard to think straight, and with Lorenzo's astonishing kiss branded on her swollen lips for all time, it was impossible. Maybe she would never think straight again. But then she wouldn't win the scholarship, Carly realised, quickly shaking herself out of it.

'All right?' Lorenzo said, looking down at her.

'Absolutely fine. Thank you for rescuing me.' She eased herself free, knowing he was only being kind.

As they reached the door two representatives from the

speed-dating company almost collided in their haste to open it for them. Lorenzo glanced at them, and then, leaning across her, held the door open for her himself. There was something about him, even without his wig and gown, that inspired fear in the heart of every wrongdoer, including her! 'If this means I'm finished I'd rather you told me straight,' she said, trying to keep up with him as he started back towards the flat.

'We'll talk about it later. Right now it's more important to get you out of this weather.' Lacing his arm through hers, he slowed, matching his pace to her shorter stride, seemingly oblivious to the sleet hitting them in the face.

'Lorenzo, I'm really sorry to bring you out on a night like this. I was just—'

'Trying to pick up a man in a bar?'

'It wasn't like that.'

'What was it like, Carly?'

'I wouldn't do anything I thought might bring chambers into disrepute.'

'Work? Is that all you think about? What about your own reputation?'

The lamplight was reflected in his eyes, making them appear to burn fiercely. The look reached inside her and twisted something. 'Lorenzo, I—'

'Lorenzo?' he interrupted. 'Do you think I have all the answers? Or maybe you think the scholarship will fill that empty space inside you? Do you even have a clue what you want out of life, Carly?'

As she stared at him in shock his jaw firmed. 'No, I didn't think so.'

As he swung an arm around her shoulder and urged her on she shrank into him, relieved that, though clearly exasperated, Lorenzo wasn't prepared to abandon her to her fate. Keeping her scholarship hopes alive was important, but meanwhile it felt good snuggling up to him, and she was going to enjoy it as long as she could. Even in the freezing cold her lips still burned from his kiss, and everywhere his hands had touched, held or stroked bore little imprints of strength and warmth and protection. Dreaming again, maybe, but it was a dream that didn't cost a broken heart to indulge in.

When they arrived back Lorenzo let them in and left her under strict instructions to strip off her clothes in the hallway. And pose nude? Catching sight of herself in the mirror, Carly quickly doused that thought. She could hear Lorenzo running a bath and, clutching her damp clothes in front of her, she draped her jacket over her shoulders for good measure.

'I thought I told you to get undressed?' he said, barely sparing her a glance.

'I am undressed…underneath…'

Zero reaction. The promise of that kiss in the bar had cooled, leaving stern Lorenzo a little sterner, but no more interested in taking her to bed than he'd ever been. This wasn't lust that ached inside her; it was something more, she realised in panic. The thought that she might have fallen in love with Lorenzo put her at more risk than a broken heart, because it made it impossible to work with him. And what about her scholarship hopes then?

'Are you coming to have your bath?' he said, distracting her. 'I'll get some towels.'

As he walked away her dreams seemed ridiculous, like the fantasies of a schoolgirl with a crush.

'Don't wait for me,' he called back.

What point would there be?

Closing her eyes, she inhaled deeply. Lorenzo was way out of her reach. Even the oil he had added to the bath water was expensive and exclusive; a man like that would never settle for anything ordinary.

This time he only put his arm round the door, brandishing thick-piled, toffee-coloured towels, each one of them big enough to swaddle her from head to foot. 'They're still warm,' he said. 'If you hang them over the radiator they'll stay that way…'

She thanked him and then settled back in the warm water so she could listen to him moving about in the kitchen. Tea and sympathy? Or maybe he was preparing a stiff drink for her to ease the news that her scholarship hopes were dashed.

'Ten minutes and then we talk,' he called to her from the hallway.

At least she didn't have long to wait to hear her fate! Relaxing back, she closed her eyes. There was little she could say in her defence. She'd been feeling low and had sought refuge in a bar, which hardly sounded like the reasoned actions of a Unicorn scholarship candidate.

Lorenzo's knock on the bathroom door made her spill bath water on the floor.

'Are you decent?'

'Yes…' Well, she was cloaked in a glittering foam blanket.

'I'm coming in.'

She sank beneath the foam.

'Drink this.'

She cautiously pushed herself back up a bit. Lorenzo was offering her a mug of warm milk. 'I hate warm milk.'

He ignored her complaint. 'Drink it while it's hot. I added honey and a sprinkling of cinnamon.'

Great. Nursery food.

'Good girl…'

She curbed the urge to spit out a milk fountain in favour of sipping slowly to see if he would stay.

'Don't move.'

It worked.

'I'm going for some more towels…'

She'd made an impression!

He returned with an armful of towels, but now it came to it he was rather more man than she could handle. Her body might be telling her to prepare for contact with some hard, tanned flesh, but she was losing her nerve.

He hunkered down.

'What are you doing?'

'Drying your hair. Maybe that way you won't catch a chill and take time off work.'

Some impression!

When Lorenzo had finished drying her hair he held out a bath sheet, allowing her to climb out of the bath with her modesty sadly intact. As if that weren't humiliating enough he told her to clean her teeth and stood aside.

Fantasies would be the death of her.

They went into her bedroom.

'Night clothes?' Lorenzo prompted.

She reached inside the bedside drawer where she stored her sexy sale bargains.

'What's that?' Lorenzo demanded as she held up a wisp of lace. 'Haven't you got anything sensible?'

Like grandma's bloomers?

'How about these?' Fishing deeper than she had, he emerged triumphantly with a pair of pink flannelette pyjamas. 'These will keep you nice and warm.'

So could he…

'Climb into bed,' he ordered, returning to the door.

This was not going to plan. This was not going anywhere. For all she knew Lorenzo might have sisters, but she didn't want to be one of them.

'Don't worry about over-sleeping. I'll wake you in the morning.'

'What about our talk?'

'We'll have it tomorrow…'

'Carly…'

'Mmm…'

'It's time to get up.'

No. He couldn't wake her now. 'Leave me,' she said grumpily. 'I'm asleep…' She had no intention of getting out of bed so soon after Lorenzo had taken so much trouble to make sure she stayed there. 'Did you have to do that?' With a groan of disapproval she tried to shield her eyes. From arrows of sunlight?

'Did I have to pull the curtains at ten o'clock in the morning? Yes, I most certainly did, young lady.'

'Ten o'clock in the morning?' Carly shot up and rubbed her eyes. The evidence was undeniable. Lorenzo was wearing his three-piece suit, and he'd shaved. He was ready for work, and the thin winter sunshine was streaming into the room.

'You've slept long enough.' His eyes narrowed. 'You wouldn't want to be late for work.'

There was an edge to his voice that suggested she had better not be.

'I won't be late.'

'Half an hour in my office.'

Half an hour? 'I'll be there.'

Last night had been his biggest test yet, and the night of the Grand Court had been the turning point in his mind between Carly Tate, promising law student, and Carly Tate, promising innumerable erotic delights. But this was question time and office time, Lorenzo reminded himself. He wanted to know more about her before writing his report for the scholarship committee. 'So, your parents are supportive?'

'Absolutely…they couldn't be more so.'

He rearranged himself in the chair. 'Do you have brothers and sisters?'

'One sister, Olivia…'

Her gaze flickered.

'Do you get on well?'

'Oh, very well. She's the pretty one.'

She gave a nervous laugh, and he wanted to tell her that he wasn't interested in pretty sisters, only Carly Tate. He had to dig deep if he was going to find out if she was committed to the programme. 'So what drew you to law?'

'It missed a generation.'

'And you felt you should fill the breach?'

'I wanted to,' she argued passionately.

'There are other worthwhile careers you could have pursued. Didn't you consider any of them?' He waited for her reply, already knowing the answer—there had only ever been one path open to her. 'How about your hobbies, Carly?'

'Hobbies?' Her eyes went blank.

'Yes, hobbies—sport, dancing, theatre—'

'Oh, I read a lot,' she interrupted.

'Law books?'

She clammed up and blushed red. She didn't want him grilling her on the latest hot reads. 'Anything else?' he pressed.

She bit her lip, drawing his attention to the other redness where his stubble had abraded her tender skin. He remembered his hackles shooting up when he'd thought the man in the bar was trying to humiliate her. He'd acted purely on instinct, but he could still remember how she'd felt beneath his hands, his mouth, and the way she'd tasted against his tongue. He wanted her now. He wanted to take her to bed right now—

'Anything else you'd like to tell me?' he said, needing the

distraction badly. But he couldn't look at her without recalling how fragile she'd been in his arms. And the thought of sinking deep into that warm, soft body—

'Do I have anything else to say?' she said, interrupting his stream of thought. She looked thoughtful. 'I want the scholarship.' Lowering her chin, she delivered him a level gaze. 'It means everything to me…'

'And to your parents too, I have no doubt…' He glanced at the door, a signal that their interview was over. He needed space.

The rest of the day flew past, not that there was much left of it. She was free to concentrate on firming up the arrangements for the Christmas party. That and ensuring Lorenzo's car was returned to him on time.

'Everything going to plan?' he said, making her heart stop when he poked his head around the door of her cubby-hole.

'Really well. Your car should be returned to you this evening.'

'And the party?'

'All going to plan.' At least something was, she thought wryly.

'Just don't be too proud to ask for my help if you need it. Will you, Carly?' Lorenzo pressed in a way that required an answer.

'Don't worry—everything's under control.'

As he pulled away from the door she spun a smile and sent it flying in his direction. She waited motionless until his footsteps had died away. It was stupid to go on feeling like this. She had to stop pining for something that was never going to happen. What she should be doing was making the hard call home—the one that told her mother she wouldn't be back for the annual gathering of the clan, because this year she had to stay in London and organise the Christmas party. 'Which, yes, Mother, includes cleaning up after it. That's right, Mother, menial tasks.' She was already rehearsing the conversation in her head. 'Someone has to do them.'

The phone call began better than Carly could have expected. Her mother was in high spirits and even swallowed her version of the party being an honour she had been entrusted with, right up to the point where she mentioned tidying up afterwards.

'Stay and clear up?' her mother exclaimed in disapproval. 'Have we paid for all that education in order for you to carry out menial tasks?'

Someone has to do them, Carly mouthed silently, and then as her mother exploded into shrill indignation she held the phone away from her ear. Her mother couldn't be expected to know what a scholarship race entailed. How you had to grovel and study until your eyes turned bright red and popped out of your head. It was better if she never knew. How could you explain that pride had no place when you were clinging on to an opportunity by your fingertips? 'Really, it's considered an honour,' Carly said during of one of her mother's rare pauses for breath.

'*An honour?* I can't see your sister agreeing to emptying slops—'

'Mum, please, it's not like that—' But her mother was in no mood for listening.

'You say yes too easily, Carly. You might be thought the clever one, but you're not shrewd or worldly-wise like Olivia. Just be sure you're not being taken for a mug. Here,' she finished impatiently. 'Speak to your father. I can't talk any sense into you. But for his sake, if nothing else, I'm asking you to rethink.'

Her father was gentler, but she could hear the disappointment in his voice. 'Dad, they're hardly likely to invite me to host the chambers party when I've so recently been granted a pupilage. Organising the Christmas party is not so bad. It's a chance to prove myself—'

'As a cleaner?' her mother prompted from the wings.

'Anyway, I'll let you know how it goes, shall I, Dad?'

Carly waited as the silence lengthened. She was longing for a word of encouragement. She heard her mother say something in the background. 'What did Mum say? I couldn't hear her.'

'She says don't eat too much at the party,' her dad reported. 'You can't afford to put on any more weight…'

CHAPTER EIGHT

'THANKS, DAD…' Carly stared at the dead receiver in her hand. Her father had been bustled off the phone because her mother wanted to make a call. She remained very still for a moment, and then emotion welled inside her. She needed air…now.

'Hey…'

Lorenzo had to move fast to avoid a collision. In her flight across Reception she'd been blind to everything, including him.

'Didn't you see me?' His lips curved up in the half smile that could turn her legs to jelly, but on this occasion seemed like one more mocking jibe.

'I saw you,' Carly lied, standing tall. She made a point of strolling to the door as if she had all the time in the world, but inside she felt like a washing machine on its final spin, whirling mindlessly, endlessly. She was frantic for space, air, rain, anything other than the claustrophobic atmosphere inside her tiny cubby-hole because that was drenched in reproach and disappointment. All she wanted was to make her parents proud, and she could never seem to do so.

Lorenzo reached across and opened the outer doors for her. 'I'm leaving too,' he said. 'Why don't we walk back together?'

She could think of a thousand reasons why she shouldn't

do that, and did her best to put him off. 'Oh, that's okay,' she said. 'I might do some shopping first.'

But he slipped into stride beside her. 'I'll worry if I leave you wandering the streets alone looking for men to kiss.'

'Last night was a one-off.'

'Okay, so if you don't want me to join you—'

'What, on my hunt for kissable men?'

Lorenzo refused to take offence. 'Kissing men has never been my style,' he said dryly.

She felt so miserable she snapped back, 'Well, I don't make a habit of it either.'

'In that case I'm glad you made an exception last night.'

Right. Lorenzo had only been trying to save her from embarrassment. He would have done the same for any of his female students. Lorenzo gave kisses easily, because kisses came easily to him; they had rarity value where she was concerned.

'Stop frowning,' he instructed, slanting a glance her way. 'Your face might stick that way. We're off duty, and even lawyers can't take themselves seriously all the time.'

Says the inquisitor-in-chief! 'So where are you heading?'

'Back to the flat. I'm going to make some supper. You can have some too. You have to eat, don't you?' he said, responding to her surprised look.

'I didn't think you could cook.'

'How many Italians do you know who don't cook?'

'I don't know many Italians.'

'Then you don't know what you're missing.'

Her cheeks blazed red on cue.

When they arrived, he suggested she take off her suit and relax. It was exactly what planned to do. It was just unfortunate as he said it that the bits of lace she kept stored in her bedroom flew into his mind. He quickly prescribed an outfit: 'Jeans and a top—something you don't mind spilling food down.' He wanted to take her to bed and it should have been straightforward, but, as he'd told his inner self before, nothing was straightforward with Carly Tate. 'My food is messy,' he said when she looked at him.

Someone had hurt her; he could see it in her eyes. So much for seduction! How could he when that same someone was putting roadblocks in his way? But the anger that surged inside him came from longing to bring her detractor to account.

'I won't be long,' she said, walking off.

Who the hell had done that to her? His work made him acutely aware of body language and she couldn't hide the strain on her face.

He went to his bedroom and took his clothes off. Hanging up his suit, he made for the bathroom. He needed a shower to clean away everything he'd seen and heard that day. Working as a criminal lawyer was all he'd ever wanted to do, but the cases he handled were real-life dramas and he could never relax until he'd washed the day away.

He felt refreshed by the time he reached the kitchen. Women loved it when he cooked. It always threw them— usually in the direction of his bed. He was a perfectionist in cooking, advocacy and sex, and knew better than most that practice made perfect. But this wasn't a cynical exercise. He was right to have doubts about Carly's future. Confidence was a prerequisite for a successful career at the bar, and it took more than a sharp brain and dedication for a student to achieve their potential. Carly carried a load of expectation on her shoulders, but what did *she* want?

'Hungry?' he said, forced to break off his cogitations when she walked into the kitchen.

'Starving,' she admitted, but then her cheeks flamed red as if she'd said something wrong.

'I promise not to poison you.'

'No need to go to any trouble—I'm not that hungry.'

'You said you were starving.'

'Are you cross-examining me, my learned friend?' She was only half joking.

'If I make it, you eat it, is that understood?' This time he was only half joking.

She blushed and looked away. To spare her the spotlight he started making a home-made salad dressing. 'To go with the pasta,' he explained, feeling pleased when she came a little closer to see what he was doing. 'Food allergies?' he queried without looking up as he added seasoning.

'None.'

'And you're not on a diet?'

Her cheeks pinked up. 'What makes you say that? Do you think I should be?'

The tone of her voice shocked him. 'No, I don't. You work long hours and you need your strength.'

Like a sumo warrior? Carly thought, watching Lorenzo wield his wooden spoon. Truthfully, she was ravenous, and this already smelled good.

'I'm going to put the dressing in the fridge,' he said, moving past her, 'and start on the tomato sauce for the pasta.'

She pressed back against the work surface. It was torture being this close to him. The jeans he'd changed into hugged his hips, and the heavy-duty belt he'd threaded through the denim loops drew her attention to things she shouldn't be sneaking looks at. Then there was the top clinging tenaciously to his hard-muscled arms.

'Taste?' he said, having beaten his sauce into submission.

She did an instant calorie calculation and agreed: tomato,

chilli and onion were safe. 'And is this your idea of a simple pasta?' It was simply delicious, that was for sure.

The look he gave her confirmed nothing was simple where Lorenzo was concerned. And then, looking for an indication of his mood, she glanced at his feet and saw they were bare. For some reason that gave her a sexual charge, which took her by surprise. Was she so desperate she was finding feet sexy now? But Lorenzo's feet *were* sexy. Tanned, with a fabulous pedicure, her eyes reported. And his hair was still damp from the shower, which she found incredibly arousing too. In fact—

'Try this now I've seasoned it again,' he said, breaking into her thoughts.

She opened her mouth as he touched the spoon to her lips.

'Better?' he said.

She licked her kiss-bruised lips, and hummed approval.

'Take a bigger mouthful. Unless you're afraid of food, of course.' He'd meant it as a joke. 'You're not, are you? Why, that's ridiculous. While I live here you're going to eat properly.'

Her stomach growled on cue, making them both laugh and relaxing the tension.

They sat down to eat. Lorenzo's ragu was rich and perfectly seasoned, and as she slowly dropped her inhibitions Carly found her tension unravelling as fast as a piece of loosely-knit cotton. 'Ice cream?' she asked, after Lorenzo had cleared their plates away and returned with dessert. She felt a moment of guilt, but only a moment. 'Oh, no, you're spoiling me.'

'It's a special Zabaglione…my own recipe. Open wide…'

It was the most indescribably delicious spoonful of food she had eaten in her life.

'The alcohol content makes the mixture soft, and so—'

She didn't listen to the rest, because Lorenzo's sleepy gaze was soothing, and the brush of his minty breath on her face was making her tender lips tingle.

'And like many things it must be eaten without delay,' he went on. 'Carly? Are you still with me?'

Barely, and yet never more so, she thought as Lorenzo dipped his head to stare her in the eyes.

'Has someone said something to upset you?'

The telephone conversation with her parents was still fresh in her mind, and the concern in Lorenzo's voice was the last straw for her tear ducts. 'No, of course not.'

'Then why are there tears in your eyes?'

'Don't be silly, there aren't any,' she said, sniffing violently. She wasn't about to reveal her weaknesses to him.

He let it go and made coffee. He put his questions down to professional interest, but it was more than that. It was new to him, this impulse to nurture. It certainly got in the way of sex for recreation. The trouble with Carly was she made him want things he couldn't have, things he didn't have time for. 'Tell me more about yourself…' He wanted to hear her speak; her voice soothed him, and right now he badly needed soothing.

'What can I tell you? I'm boring,' she said.

'Why don't you let me be the judge of that?'

'Another test? I thought we were off duty?'

'These are scholarship questions,' he lied.

'How am I doing?' Her eyes fired.

He didn't want to answer that. He wasn't prepared to commit himself either way. Carly was a strong candidate. On paper, at least. Or was that being unfair to her, because he wanted her in his bed?

It was more than that, Lorenzo reflected. He doubted Carly's commitment to the scholarship programme. She had allowed herself to believe she wanted nothing more on earth than the Unicorn scholarship, but in his view her motives were wrong. The scholarship was a prize she'd take home for her parents like an eager puppy might take a ball. He doubted she'd thought further than the winner's name being announced. Where the Unicorn would take her was immaterial, it was where it would take her parents that obsessed Carly. 'So, what's the boyfriend situation?' he said to distract them both. And, yes, because he wanted to know. He had an obsession too—the thought of sex with Carly, and right now it was driving him hard.

'There isn't one,' she said, turning on a frank stare. 'I don't have time.'

Should that answer please him quite so much? 'So you won't be leaving anyone behind if you're awarded the scholarship?'

Only you... With a head and heart full of Lorenzo it wasn't easy to stare straight at him and convince them both there was no one she cared about. 'No one,' she repeated, avoiding his gaze.

'Surely your parents have someone lined up for you?'

'Maybe, but I didn't approve of their selection.'

'You make them sound like a box of chocolates.'

'That's just what they were,' she agreed. 'But they were all strawberry creams, when I was looking for—'

'Bitter chocolate and a hard nut?' he suggested dryly.

'Exactly...' She looked at him, wishing the comparison between men with grey socks and darkly, dangerous Lorenzo could have been a little less extreme. 'Anyway—'

'Anyway?'

'Like I said before, I don't have time for men.' It was a useful lie. 'The speed-dating fiasco was a mistake. I found myself in the right place at the wrong time, and then I just got swept away by the prospect of—'

'Sharing a man's bed with countless others?'

'No!'

He hummed sceptically as he might have done in court. 'Are you sure your parents don't know what's best for you?'

He poured coffee, but she wondered at the tense line of his jaw. 'I'm positive.' She passed the cream. 'So-called society can be incredibly dull.'

He sat back. 'Tell me about it.'

'Bores who think their stories are irresistible, and when you try to get to know them, you wonder why you—'

He cut in. 'I didn't mean tell me literally, I was agreeing with you.'

'You were?'

'Yes, I was, Carly.'

Well, that had to be a first! The way Lorenzo was looking at her now was unfathomable. The only thing she could say for sure was that it made her heart melt.

She would get over him and get on with her life, Carly told herself firmly. This little chat was nothing more than a fishing expedition on Lorenzo's part so he could write a proper report. 'Thanks for taking the time to talk to me.' She was just congratulating herself on a great exit line when she missed her footing and landed in his arms.

'Bed?' he suggested.

She stared into his eyes, hardly daring to breathe.

'I need you back working full tilt tomorrow.'

Ah.

He steadied her back on her feet and said goodnight. She'd almost made it out of the room when he added, 'Your parents must be very proud of you.'

'Yes, of course they are.' She stiffened.

'And this scholarship would mean a lot to them?'

'Of course…'

'And to you?'

When she didn't reply immediately, he added, 'I should

think they're already proud of you. You don't need the Unicorn scholarship on top of everything else.'

Her stomach clenched. Was Lorenzo trying to tell her something? If he was she'd rather he just came out and say it. 'Lorenzo, please don't mess me about—I'd rather know.'

'And you know I can't tell you my decision.'

She gripped the door handle for a moment and then left the room. He fought the urge to go after her. He had been trying to let her down lightly and he'd messed up. He waited until she shut her bedroom door and then only managed to stop himself punching the wall because it wasn't his wall to punch.

He was suspended between business and pleasure with a bridge of lust in between. If he had been searching for a recipe for disaster, he couldn't have found a better one.

CHAPTER NINE

ONLY ONE MORE NIGHT until Carly's Christmas party. That was her second thought as she woke up. The first—since it contained Lorenzo—was censored.

There was a street lamp outside the window shedding a grudging light inside the room. She lay in bed staring at the ceiling, telling herself she was stealing the last few moments in a warm bed before getting up, when really she was listening for Lorenzo. And fretting. He had dug and dug last night until she'd given up who knew what innermost secrets. One thing was for sure: he'd read more into what she'd said than anyone who wasn't a top-flight barrister might. She wasn't fooled for a minute by his cosy chit-chat; he'd been using his tried-and-tested courtroom technique to find out everything he could about her. So had she blown her scholarship chances out of the water? Only Lorenzo knew that, and he wasn't telling.

It shouldn't be hard to avoid him today she'd be so busy, but it was when they were both home like this and the apartment hummed with his energy she found it so difficult to relax. How long would it take to fix a leak at his flat? When would she be rid of him?

Who was she trying to kid? She was aching for sex; aching for Lorenzo.

Burying her head under the pillows, she tried to shut out the sound of his shower running. The thought of him naked beneath the spray was nothing short of torment, but, short of a miracle, aching for sex was how she was going to stay. Lorenzo Domenico might be the hottest thing on two hard-muscled legs, but he wasn't interested in her.

The bathroom grew silent again. Sitting up in bed, she hugged her knees, resting her chin. The best thing to do was work twice as hard to prove to Lorenzo that her parents' expectations weren't the only thing driving her.

Lifting the envelope containing Carly's lists, he picked up the phone and summoned her. Minutes later she was in his office.

He eased back in his chair, acting as if the sight of her had no effect on his libido. 'Let's go over these lists,' he said, handing her the copies.

Lists plural? He had *both* her lists?

'Lists?' she squeaked, delving frantically through her memory bank. She distinctly remembered stuffing Lorenzo's list inside an envelope and popping it inside his pigeon-hole. She knew it was his envelope because she had marked it For Your Eyes Only. For one look into Lorenzo's eyes she would do a lot of things...but not, *surely,* mix up her lists?

'You put an envelope into my pigeon-hole, didn't you?' he said, confirming it was all right to relax. But then a suspicious curve tugged at his lips. 'And I picked this list up when you dropped it...'

He'd got the wrong envelope! It wasn't just a list she'd dropped, it was the bottom out of her world!

'Is it getting too hot for you?' Lorenzo murmured as she eased the neck of her shirt. 'I can easily turn the central heating down.'

He could turn the air-conditioning up and it wouldn't

impact on her discomfort. Toughing it out was the only way
left to her. She played it cool. 'Oh, *that* list. I still have one
or two additions to make, so if you wouldn't mind…' She held
out her hand in a way that would make any normal person act
immediately.

'Additions?' Lorenzo said dryly. 'Can it be possible you've
left something out?'

Her cheeks fired as she thought about it. Her cravings, her
fantasies of everything she'd like Lorenzo to do to her—all of
them written down in note form, some with explicit doodles…

'No, I didn't think so,' he said. 'I think you'd better explain
yourself, Carly.'

Inwardly, she shrank. Explain what? That she wanted to go
to bed with Lorenzo—and not once, but many times, and each
of those times was going to be more inventive than the last—

'I hope you haven't circulated this list to your colleagues,'
he said, showing a distinct absence of humour.

'No, of course not!' That was the one thing she could be
sure about. The list Lorenzo had just placed on the desk in
front of him was one of a kind.

'Good,' he said evenly. 'It could corrupt in the wrong
hands…'

Forget toughing it out! 'Sorry.' Snatching the list off his
desk, she ran out. If she was going down she was going down
with all guns blazing!

Back home that night, wanting to take her mind off Lorenzo,
and inspired by his prowess in the kitchen, Carly baked a
cake. And not just any cake. A cake decorated with emerald-
green icing. The bottle of colouring had been tiny, the bowl
large—who knew you were supposed to put in a drop of
green colouring and not the whole bottle?

In spite of this small setback she decided stubbornly

that it would make an excellent centrepiece for the buffet table at the Christmas party.

'Emerald-green icing?' Madeline stared.

'It's festive,' Carly pointed out. She had drawn quite a crowd on her arrival in chambers, and was prepared to defend the first cake she had ever baked to hell and back again.

'It will brighten up the buffet table no end,' one of the clerks agreed. 'You could use it for a centrepiece.'

'That's the plan…' She was smiling again by the time she replaced the lid on the tin.

'You have got everything ready for tonight, haven't you, Carly?' Madeline asked anxiously as everyone peeled away. 'Only Lorenzo went off to court like a bear with a sore head—'

'Did he…?' she asked, trying to sound indifferent while she inwardly groaned. This was it. She was finished. After the encounter in his office and the wretched list she should have expected it. 'Of course I'm ready.' She changed track quickly, seeing Madeline's suspicious nose was already twitching at the thought of something juicy to spread around.

'What will you wear?' Madeline gave her the quick up and down.

She wasn't falling for that one again. 'I haven't decided yet,' Carly replied vaguely, her mind on other things—like the tirade of anger due from Lorenzo.

'Don't you think you should?' Madeline demanded with a frown, taking a large bite out of a succulent Krispie Kreme. 'Want one?' she offered, holding out the box. She didn't just offer, she held the box stuffed with freshly-baked doughnuts right under Carly's nose. 'I didn't have time to stop for breakfast,' Madeline explained as the mouth-wateringly sugary smell invaded Carly's quivering nostrils.

Carly's stomach growled in disappointment as she refused the offer. But what could she do? She had nine hours to drop a dress size, and no intention of squandering a single minute. 'I had breakfast before I left the flat, thank you,' she lied glibly. 'And now, if you will excuse me, Madeline, I really should be getting on…'

'Of course…' Madeline looked curiously at the hefty brief beneath Carly's arm, tied ostentatiously as all briefs were supposed to be with bright pink ribbon. The sight of it didn't have quite the same effect on Madeline as the box of Krispy Kremes had had on Carly, but at least it made Madeline's predatory gaze narrow, which was something.

'Lorenzo entrusts you with his briefs?'

'I'm looking this one over for him, actually,' Carly said, excusing her fib on the grounds of extreme provocation. The truth was Lorenzo had left the papers behind in the flat, and she thought he might need them. And returning them was as good an excuse to see him again and beg for his mercy.

'What about your dress for tonight, Carly?' Madeline pressed.

'Who said anything about a dress?'

'You surely can't be thinking of turning up in trousers?' Madeline looked fit to faint.

'Now, Madeline, you know that everything about the Christmas party is supposed to be a surprise.'

'A surprise, not a shock,' Madeline pointed out, taking another monster bite from her doughnut. 'But if you should need any help…'

And see you coming? I'll run a mile, Carly thought, smiling sweetly as she pressed the elevator call button. She had enough trouble on her hands as it was.

'Only I saw this dress, and it's just you—'

Carly breathed a sigh of relief as the elevator doors closed right on cue.

Carly smiled with satisfaction. She was ready. She had arranged for everything to be delivered at least two hours before it would be needed for the party, and so far her plan was running like clockwork. Everyone else had gone home at lunchtime to prepare. She hadn't managed to see Lorenzo, which she told herself was a good thing as she plonked the brief down on his desk. Actually, it was; she was anxious enough. She had warned the security guard at Reception that no one, apart from her suppliers, was to come anywhere near the main hall. If she was going down, she was going down with the most spectacular bang.

How could you go without food for a whole day and still not lose weight? Having raced back to the flat, Carly was now struggling with the skirt she had planned to wear for the party—black lace over a flesh-coloured skirt. If you didn't look too closely, it gave the illusion of lace over naked skin—though whatever had possessed her to imagine anyone would want to see her naked flesh escaped her now. Tugging it off, she discarded it on top of the ever-growing clothes mountain at the foot of her bed.

She was getting desperate, but then she noticed the snow drifting past the window. Snow was good news, because snow made it possible to pile on layers which, hopefully, would conceal everything underneath. Plus, if she transformed herself into something shapeless and sexless, no one would care how much she ate. Brilliant. When she wasn't handing out food she could be eating it.

There was a far bigger turnout than Carly had expected, and everyone was in party mood, including Madeline.

'Carly, you're a star!' Madeline enthused, managing at the same time to frown with incredulity that Carly could have achieved something so enjoyable. 'Everyone's saying that no one but you would have had the nerve to put on a Northern night.'

'Really?' Was that good, or bad? Carly wondered. And where was Lorenzo? She gazed around nervously. The sooner they could have their confrontation and get it over with, the better. She knew she was finished. She just didn't know the mode of execution Lorenzo would choose to despatch her with yet.

'I can see now why you didn't need my fashion advice,' Madeline commented with a critical gaze. 'How clever of you to get that grunge outfit exactly right.'

'Thank you,' Carly said, trying not to chip her teeth in the process of grinding her jaw into the approximation of a smile.

'I'm having such fun,' Madeline confided. 'Beer and skittles! Who'd have thought you could come up with such an original idea?'

'Have you seen Lorenzo?'

'Oh…' Madeline's face took on a concerned look. 'Did I forget to say? He asked to see you in his office the moment you showed your face…'

The *moment* she showed her face? This was bad. 'So he's here?' It was too late to hide her feelings from Madeline. Her guard was down, and everything she felt about him, all the longing and apprehension, was on her face for everyone to see.

'He's been here for some time…monitoring the situation,' Madeline said ominously. 'There's nothing for you to worry about. You just have to accept that a man like Lorenzo isn't used to this kind of entertainment. I'm sure he'll get over it.'

'Is he very angry?'

'Who knows? Lorenzo never shows his feelings. Surely you've learned that by now?'

If nothing else? Carly wondered, maintaining a neutral expression as she crunched on Madeline's barb.

Madeline shrugged. 'But never mind. At least I'm enjoying your party…' She gave Carly a consoling hug, dropping a greasy sausage-and-onion kiss on the cheek for good measure. 'Can't stop!' she exclaimed happily, having wrought the appropriate level of havoc on Carly's nerves. 'Must go and sign up for the snooker tournament.'

Carly's insides were lashing about like crazy, but there was no escape. Whatever anyone thought there was only one person who mattered, and he was waiting to see her in his office.

She should have known Lorenzo would be here from the start. She should have known he wouldn't like this sort of casual, rowdy party. And on top of everything else that had happened it was the final straw; the straw that proved she had made a complete hash of things.

Carly elbowed her way across a crowded dance floor as she attempted to reach the corridor where the seniors' offices were located. She gleaned some comfort from the fact that the dance floor was crowded with judges and QCs, all jiggling about. At least they were having fun. She hadn't been able to afford a DJ and so she had hired a beat-up jukebox from a friend of Madame Xandra's. The skittles had been thrown in along with a dartboard and a snooker table, as well as several boxes of dominoes and Shove Halfpenny boards, which were being fought over this very minute. When she had queried the minuscule cost of so much entertainment, Madame Xandra had explained that retro was finished. Maybe it was, but the legal world was centuries behind, meaning that for most of her guests retro had barely arrived.

As she walked briskly down the corridor towards her fate she tried to picture Lorenzo in his sober three-piece suit throwing darts… It wasn't easy; in fact, she failed.

What had she been thinking?

* * *

She hesitated briefly, and then rapped firmly on Lorenzo's door.

'Come in.'

Seated behind his desk he looked suitably stern.

'Before you say anything—'

'I'd like to congratulate you,' he said, ignoring her. 'Your party's a huge success.'

There was a 'but' in there somewhere; there had to be. His face gave nothing away. 'Did I do something wrong?'

'I'd be happier if it weren't for this.' He held out the list.

'I can only apologise…' Not prepared to give up yet, she sidled up to his desk and tried to take it.

He lifted it out of her reach. 'Shut the door, please,' he said briskly.

A sense of failure swept over her as she closed the door. A black cloud sat on her head as she thought about her parents and the disappointment that was about to envelop them.

Lorenzo remained seated, remained stern. She bit her lip and then bit back tears. However hard she tried, she always let people down. 'I'm sorry,' she started, but then, just as she began to speak she had a vision of Madeline Du Pre gloating. It was time to stop feeling sorry for herself and defend her corner. 'I did my best,' she said robustly, 'and if you don't like it—'

'I can what?' Lorenzo challenged in a lazy voice, unfolding from his chair.

She swayed back. How could she have forgotten how big he was? Was every bit of him in proportion? She reddened as her thoughts ran riot. He towered over her. Ominously.

'What are you wearing?' He came a step closer.

Did it matter? Did he care? Would anyone notice what she was wearing when she left the building? And at least she was warm, which was something! 'It was snowing outside when I left the flat—'

'But that's hardly a party outfit,' Lorenzo commented, viewing it disparagingly. 'You're hot,' he said.

Obviously! But then she noticed the look in his eyes and blushed. Did he mean what she thought he meant? 'Really?' she said in a different voice.

'Absolutely. Now, I think we should make a start by removing some of these layers… This shawl, for instance,' he said, unwinding it, 'is quite unnecessary in a centrally heated building.'

'I didn't have time to take it off,' she stuttered as he tossed it aside. 'Look, I know I'm not hot on fashion, but—'

'But what?' he said. 'You've cornered the market in cardigans?'

Okay, maybe she had added one too many. She gasped as first one cardigan and then another hit the floor.

'Or caftans, perhaps?' he said, fingering the heavy cloth of the garment she was wearing underneath.

'This isn't a caftan,' she said with affront. 'This is a genuine beaded *abaya* from the souk. I only bought it last year—'

'Well, it looks like a Bedouin tent to me. Are you sure you bought it from a clothes stall?'

'Quite sure…' She gasped as he lifted it over her head.

'This won't do, Ms Tate. Apart from your rotten taste in clothes, you've broken the first rule on your list. Or was it the second?' Rasping the stubble on his chin, he thought about it. 'You do remember the rule to which I'm referring?'

'Of course I do.' She drew with relief upon her flawless memory bank, which unlike her social skills and doodling, never let her down. '"Arrive early,"' she quoted, '"and make a point of speaking to your immediate superior—"'

'But you didn't make a point of speaking to your immediate superior. I was waiting here to see you.'

Her breath rushed out in shock as Lorenzo started undoing

the laces at the neck of the traditional shirt she was wearing underneath her abaya.

'Now this is an ugly thing,' he said, 'so we'll discard it.'

'I'm really, *really* sorry.' She glanced anxiously at the growing mound of clothes. 'I'll get some help—a personal shopper…a full make-over—'

'Let's forget your fashion crisis for now,' Lorenzo soothed, 'and concentrate on your rules.' He referred to the list again, while she could think of nothing other than the lurid activities her matchstick people had indulged in.

'I like this rule,' he said, looking up. Lorenzo's eyes were so dark they were almost black. 'You must remain visible and maintain a pleasant and interested smile on your face at all times… Well?' he prompted softly. 'What do you have to say about that, Ms Tate?'

She gasped again as the first of her vests hit the floor.

CHAPTER TEN

'I WROTE THOSE GUIDELINES at your instruction,' Carly reminded Lorenzo in a voice that refused to stop trembling. 'Just like you said, they're meant to help the less experienced members of chambers in stressful party conditions—'

'And are they helping you?' he said in a murmur as he peeled off another vest.

'Lorenzo…what are you doing?' She eased her neck, subconsciously presenting it for his attention…

'You don't know?'

Lorenzo's face was very close to her ear. His warm breath was making it tingle, and she gave a little groan.

'Are you cooler yet?'

Was he joking?

He was so close now the harsh cut of his beard grazed her skin, and before she had chance to recover from that he licked her ear.

'Shall I stop?' he said when she trembled.

Only if you want to, she wanted to say, but her lips moved and no sound came out—other than a ragged sigh that was half a moan. 'Don't you dare,' she managed to force out.

He backed her up against the door, taking it slowly,

crossing the room step by inevitable step, until she could feel the cool wood against her back and he could reach the lock.

'Exactly how many garments are you wearing?' he murmured, perusing them.

'Quite a few yet…' Suddenly all those layers seemed more of a blessing than a curse; the unwrapping process made her wish she'd put on more.

'You must be steaming,' Lorenzo growled against her ear.

He had no idea!

'The best thing we can do,' he said, 'is remove everything…'

'What about the party?'

'The best parties run themselves…and you have put on an excellent party.'

'What a relief…'

'Indeed. Now…is this a thermal vest?'

'One of two,' she admitted.

'Will you take it off, or shall I?'

Reaching up, she hesitated a second, and then instead of taking her vest off she loosened his tie.

Lorenzo cocked his head to one side with a slow smile burning. 'Why, Ms Tate, that's very forward of you…'

'I think I'm beginning to get the hang of this.'

'I always knew you were a good student.' He whipped off her vest as she pushed his jacket from his shoulders.

'Now, this is very nice,' Lorenzo approved, discovering another of her lucky sale finds in silk, lace and satin.

Teasing him, she crossed her arms over her *décolletage*. The aquamarine camisole, which was her very last top, thank goodness, was so fine it hid nothing.

'How interesting,' Lorenzo observed softly, 'that in spite of wearing everything else you possess you have forgotten to put on a bra.'

'They're so confining.'

'At last, we agree—' his lips tugged at one corner and his eyes lit with humour as he gazed down at her '—but I should warn you that inappropriate behaviour at the Christmas party can seriously limit your career.'

'While expert schmoozing without resorting to being a creep helps you to move up the ladder,' Carly retorted with a look that was almost as wicked as Lorenzo's.

Taking hold of her arms, he removed them gently but firmly from her chest and placed them at her side, drawing a soft moan from her lips as he ran the tips of his nails very lightly down them. 'That list was an excellent piece of work,' he commended huskily. 'It gave me all sorts of pointers as to what you might like—'

'Did you need them?'

Lorenzo was concentrating on stroking her breasts beneath the filmy fabric and didn't welcome her interruption. 'Not really,' he murmured, without looking up. She groaned as he moved on to tease the tip of her nipples with his thumbnails.

'Watch out for horns,' he reminded her when she reached up to lace her fingers through his hair.

'You read the wrong list,' she complained.

'I read every list,' Lorenzo husked against her lips. 'Surely you know by now how very thorough I am?'

'I'm counting on it…'

He backed her up towards an intricately inlaid Linley table, positioned at a convenient height against the wall. He lifted her onto it. 'My only complaint—'

'Yes?' she said anxiously.

'Is that I can think of a much better use for a table than dancing on top of it.'

'Merry nights make sad mornings…' Carly warned.

'Not necessarily,' Lorenzo countered, his hands running down her torso to her thighs.

Her fingers flew down his shirt studs and sent them flying, and while he was otherwise occupied she ripped his shirt off too. He teased her with almost kisses, making suggestions based on her doodles in between, while she pulled down his zip. His low, husky voice had made her wild for him, as did the expression in his eyes. And his chest…she explored it greedily. It was like polished bronze, like a statue by Michelangelo, and his body was made for sin…

As her camisole floated to the floor they fell on each other like starving men at a banquet. Lorenzo tasted great, and she did too, judging by the way his kisses were migrating down her neck. The kiss in the bar had been nothing compared to this; she'd been constrained by convention when they were in public, but now, when she was alone with him—

Carly gasped with disappointment when Lorenzo stopped touching her abruptly to rip open a foil packet.

'So you're…'

'Not a virgin,' she confirmed happily, shrieking with excitement when his warm hands cupped her buttocks. 'But you were a Boy Scout,' she asserted as he settled her in position.

'A Boy Scout?'

'Be prepared?' she reminded him.

'I would certainly recommend it,' he advised, nudging his way between her thighs.

Lovely desk, wonderful desk, perfect desk, it was just the right height. She was completely at his mercy now, naked, available, and panting for release. 'Oh…!' she breathed in a long-drawn-out ecstatic sigh.

'Delicious,' Lorenzo murmured, testing her.

'Delicious?' she breathed against his hard, warm, naked chest.

'You're plump in all the right places, and juicy like a fig—'

'I swear if you stop now… If you start to tease me, or make me wait—'

'You'll what?'

'Oh, Lorenzo!' The breath shot out of her as he plunged deep.

'You approve?'

'You know I do,' Carly gasped, grinding her fingers into Lorenzo's buttocks to urge him on. 'I've waited long enough—' Her voice broke off and then came back again, but this time without words and in a series of fractured shrieks. He was moving faster now, thrusting into her efficiently while holding her in place.

She should have known when she first saw his feet, Carly reasoned wildly. If feet were any indicator Lorenzo should have been huge, but he was even bigger than that, and most importantly he knew what to do with it. 'Oh, you're good…' Groaning with pleasure, she let her head fall back. She had started out quite prepared to take an active part, but with a man like this the wisest thing was to relax into it, and allow him to amaze her.

Which he did.

She had no idea any man could stretch her like this and massage every part of her at once. Lorenzo was hot, hard, huge and incredible. 'You're incredible!' she moaned, to which he replied by grinding his hips round and round. 'That's amazing!' Another shriek.

'I'm only taking your advice that first impressions count.' He rotated his hips again and again.

'Oh, they do, they do,' she yelped again, writhing greedily against him. 'Just…don't…be tempted to leave the building,' she managed to gasp out.

'When I leave, I leave with you,' he said, holding her safe as she grew frantic with excitement.

'I can't hold back.'

'You're not supposed to.'

She worked her hips to match each of his powerful thrusts, digging her fingers into him and sinking her teeth into his shoulder like a wildcat. 'Faster! Faster!' she ordered him, until the climax hit her and she was powerless to resist. It was bigger than anything she'd ever known, all-consuming, and massive, extraordinary, wonderful.

It took for ever for the pleasure waves to subside, and when they did she slumped against him.

'Better now?' he asked her.

'Getting there,' she admitted cautiously in case there was any more.

Tilting her chin so he could look into her eyes, Lorenzo brushed her mouth with his lips and kissed her deeply again.

'Did you mean it?' she said when he pulled back.

'Did I mean what?'

'What you said about us leaving together?'

'I've never been more serious in my life,' Lorenzo whispered, and, cupping her face in both his hands, he kissed her again.

He made her feel special. But she shouldn't get used to it. This was Lorenzo and Carly Tate. 'I mustn't keep you from the party—'

Lorenzo shushed her by placing a finger over her swollen lips, and then he replaced his finger with his mouth and kissed her into oblivion again. She was lost in an erotic haze but even something this good had to end.

'I'd better get out there,' he said.

'Must you?'

Lorenzo laughed.

He wanted nothing more than to yield to temptation. It was the best sex he'd ever had. Ever. Carly Tate was everything he'd imagined and more. *Caro Dio!* She was a real woman with real breasts and real hips; she had everything, including an appetite that matched his own. She was perfect, better than perfect, and this wasn't the end, it was just the beginning. After a feast like that he couldn't wait to get her into bed and for the banquet to begin.

But unfortunately they had to get back to the party. 'Why don't you take a shower in my bathroom,' he suggested, punctuating the words with kisses, 'while I use the staff facilities?' He smiled down at her, loving everything about her—the look in her eyes, the touch of her soft skin against his, her warmth, especially her warmth. 'And then we'll go back to the party together, and celebrate your triumph…'

She was in such a state of bliss it took her a moment when she shut the bathroom door to notice what was hanging on the back of it. As she took it in her heart stopped beating, and all the strength drained from her body. How could anyone be so cruel? 'Lorenzo…' Her angry voice shook.

'Yes?' he called back, sounding completely unconcerned.

'What is this?' Carly demanded, flinging the door open. She couldn't bring herself to look at him. She refused to believe he could be such a monster.

'What on earth's the matter with you, Carly?'

She was determined not to cry or lose her cool, and so instead she tilted her head towards the fabulous Chloe dress hanging on the back of the door, still in its clear Cellophane wrapper. To add insult to injury, it was the most beautiful dress she had ever seen. Low-necked in a clear blue silk, it had a defined waist and spaghetti straps, and a skirt that was softly flaring and would fall just below the knee. It was a dream of a dress, a dress that only a beautiful and slender woman would wear.

Lorenzo frowned at her. 'Don't you like it?'

Her response sounded like an animal in pain.

'It's not that bad, is it?' he said incredulously, coming closer to look. 'I spent a long time choosing it, but if you don't think it's right—'

'Right for what, Lorenzo?' she managed to choke out.

'Right for you,' he said, as if that were obvious. 'Look, it's no big deal. If you don't like it I won't be offended. Wear it tonight, and then throw it away.'

'No, just a minute…say that again.'

'Say what again?'

She wanted to wind back time over and over, and hear him say it a thousand times. 'The dress is for me?'

'Well, there's no one else here,' he said, 'and I'm certainly not going to wear it.'

But what if it didn't fit? He'd bought her a dress; he'd gone to all that trouble just for her? And it wasn't just any dress, but the most beautiful dress in the world… Of course it wouldn't fit. She went hot and cold at the prospect of trying it on. Clothes like this were made for thin, elegant women… She threw an anxious glance at it and then looked away. She couldn't bear to see it. She dreaded the look of disappointment on Lorenzo's face when he realised that the dress wouldn't even make it over her breasts, let alone her hips.

'Take your shower,' he said, 'and then call me in if you have any trouble putting the dress on.'

She'd rather die and was already looking for a window wide enough to climb through.

'There are some shoes over in the corner to go with it.'

Her cheeks blazed as she stared at them… They were gorgeous too. 'You guessed the size of my feet?' She blushed scarlet; size yeti.

'No…' He came back and caressed her face, making her look at him. 'I went into your bedroom and checked.'

Of course!

'What's the problem?' he said. 'You're going to look beautiful. Or is that a problem? Do you still want to hide yourself away beneath bundles of old clothes? I think it's time to show off that fabulous figure and walk tall at my side in five-inch heels.'

'I'm already tall,' she pointed out. And her mother had advised that flat shoes were the best option, because no man wanted a woman to tower over him.

'I'll still be taller than you,' Lorenzo told her. Taking hold of her shoulders, he drew her in front of him. 'Carly,' he murmured, staring into her eyes. 'You're beautiful. Why can't you believe that?' He tipped up her chin, making her look at him. 'You are not going to tie your gorgeous hair into a knot, and you *are* going to wear the dress and shoes I have chosen for you. And if I tell you you're beautiful, then that's what you are. All you have to do is believe...'

He kissed her brow, her eyes, her lips... 'You're beautiful,' he said again. '*Siete una donna giovane bella...* Now go and take that shower or people will wonder where we've got to.' As usual he made no attempt to hide his wicked smile. 'Go,' he said, urging her into his private bathroom. 'I'll take the staff bathroom, and I'll be back in a few minutes to help you dress...'

After she had showered, Carly stared at the fabulous dress beneath its polythene cover. She'd left her hair down as Lorenzo had requested, so that it floated round her naked shoulders. The bronze and copper curls seemed to have taken on a life of their own, and it was a life that defied her attempts to scrape it back and flatten it down. She had even put the shoes on...and was sure she was now about ten feet tall. She felt as if it was her first day in court, or the day she sat her first exam, or—

'Oh, to hell with it!' Carly exclaimed, ripping the dress

from its hanger. If she was going to be humiliated she might as well get it over with.

The designer gown fluttered over Carly's naked skin like a caress. The fabric settled on her curves as if it had been fitted properly in a couturier's atelier. The colour couldn't have provided a better foil for her auburn hair, and the length was perfect. She stared at her reflection in astonishment. She was transformed. She had never worn a party dress in her life before. She had never shopped for one. Why would she? She had never worn anything that embraced her figure rather than concealing it.

'Can I come in yet?' Lorenzo called.

Opening the door a crack, she put her face close to it. 'I can't manage the zip—' The moment she spoke she wished she hadn't. Would it even do up?

Lorenzo opened the door fully and stood, staring at her.

'Will I do?' she asked nervously.

'*Buon cielo!*' he exclaimed. 'Did I say you were beautiful? I lied. You are exquisite. You are the most beautiful woman I have ever seen. Where have you been hiding yourself, Carly Tate?'

'I'm not sure if the zip will fasten up.'

Placing his hands on her shoulders, Lorenzo dropped a reverent kiss on the nape of her neck as he reached behind her. 'It fastens easily,' he said. 'The dress fits you perfectly as I knew it would. And now I'm going to be the proudest man at the party, and everyone will envy me…'

'You're the kindest man I know.'

'Kind?' he said wryly. 'Someone should tell you there's a degree of self-interest when a man buys a beautiful woman a gift.' His smile eased into a grin. 'Well, what are you waiting for?'

As he offered her his arm she caught a flash of the kingfisher silk lining beneath his sober three-piece suit. His socks would be equally exotic. What was a man like this doing with her? He was so different from every other man. He was so dazzling, he blinded her. Lorenzo dared to be different. He dared. And that was what she loved about him…

She loved him, Carly realised with a jolt. It wasn't just in her imagination as she had thought. She loved Lorenzo. She had fallen in love with Lorenzo Domenico.

CHAPTER ELEVEN

'OH, NO, LOOK at my cake.' Carly stared in dismay at the buffet table.

'It looks fine to me.' Lorenzo ran a hand through his shower-damp hair.

'You look fine to me, but the cake doesn't,' Carly argued, darting a glance around to make sure they weren't being overheard.

Lorenzo's eyes warmed with a new familiarity. 'Carly?' he said, removing a strand of hair from her love-stained lips. 'Try and concentrate, will you?'

'That's exactly what I am doing,' she insisted, holding his gaze.

'On the party,' he reminded her. 'I want you to see how well it's going. Look,' he said, turning her to see as another colleague squeezed past them with a loaded plate of food. 'It's a huge success.'

'Unlike my cake,' she said, grimacing. 'No one's brave enough to try a slice of green cake.'

'I am.'

'But it's oozing unattractively beneath the lights.'

'All the more reason to eat it quickly,' Lorenzo pointed out, squeezing her arm. 'I'm sure it will taste fantastic. Why don't you cut me a slice, and let me start a trend?'

The cake almost made it as far as the plate, but then she dropped it. As she was crouching down to clear up the mess Lorenzo joined her. 'I'm sorry,' she said.

'For what?'

For being clumsy, for not sticking to her diet, for not remembering to cover her freckles with fake tan before she set out for the party this evening…

The list went on and on. But most of all she was sorry she was determined to believe everything Lorenzo said when it could only end in tears. 'For not being a better baker,' she fudged, realising he was still waiting for her answer.

'There are classes for things like that,' he said dismissively. Springing up he cut a slice of cake, and then proceeded to feed her.

'No more, please,' she begged, fearing for her disappearing waistline.

'I don't want to risk you shrinking away.'

'No danger of that,' she said self-consciously.

'Haven't you noticed the way people are staring at you?'

'They're wondering why I've changed my clothes, that's all,' she said, turning to glance around.

'I don't think so,' Lorenzo disagreed. 'They think, as I do, that it's great to see you happy and great to see you looking so lovely and so loved…'

'Loved?' She laughed and made a joke of it. 'I'd hardly win a popularity poll here.'

'Oh, I don't know,' Lorenzo argued.

She looked round in embarrassment, hoping no one had heard him. 'If you carry on like this I won't be able to get my head out of the door.'

'I think we've got a long way to go before we reach that stage,' he said. 'But in the meantime, Carly, why don't you enjoy your triumph?'

* * *

At the end of the evening the party was declared a success, just as Lorenzo had predicted. Everyone said that in future all social events must be left for Carly to arrange.

As for Carly, she had just one regret and that was if she won the Unicorn scholarship she wouldn't be around to organise anything. It had surprised her to discover how much she had enjoyed the challenge of arranging the Christmas party, and in no way did she see it beneath her, or a menial task. How could she, when it had brought pleasure to so many people? Plus it was a way to get to know them better, which she'd never had the confidence to do before.

'You worked a miracle tonight,' Lorenzo told her as they walked home together. 'You took my measly budget and turned it into something everyone will talk about for years to come.'

'I'm not sure I can top my Northern night.'

'You don't have to. You'll think of something else for the next time, and whatever you do will be well received. Tonight's triumph will become your badge of honour, your success story by which you will be known from now on.'

'You talk as if there's going to be no more law.'

'You can do whatever you want to do,' he told her in a voice that had suddenly turned serious.

Alarm bells sounded, but she didn't want to break the easy mood between them by raising the spectre of the Unicorn scholarship. 'You make it all sound easy, so romantic.'

'You know me better than that, Carly. An event planner couldn't have done better than you did tonight. I'm just pointing out that the world's your oyster. Now stop fumbling with the lock and give me that key.'

'You're impatient.'

'There are some things that can't wait, and you're one of them—'

But the first thing Carly saw when Lorenzo opened the front door was a letter from her mother sitting on the mat.

'Leave that now,' he said, dragging her close so he could bury his face in her hair.

At first she couldn't stop thinking about it. She was far too tense as she held the letter in her hand, but Lorenzo took matters, or, rather, Carly, into his own hands, and made her forget.

Tugging off their clothes as they ran, they laughed and tumbled their way down the hallway. Carly was heading for her bedroom, but Lorenzo cut her off at the pass. 'My room,' he insisted, swinging her into his arms. 'The bed's bigger, and we're going to need every inch of it.'

A bed! A real bed! Oh, bliss. She threw herself down on top of it, making Lorenzo laugh. She didn't care what he thought, she only knew she wanted him. Reaching up, she demanded he kiss her without further delay. The blue dress had clearly worked some magic, because he took her in his arms and told her she was beautiful again.

'Okay, okay,' he murmured as she laced her fingers through his hair and tugged. He dropped a kiss on her swollen mouth. 'I get the message…'

'But not quickly enough,' she complained.

The gorgeous silky dress floated to the floor with her lacy thong, and then the bed dipped as Lorenzo came to lie down beside her.

'I can't,' she said in a moment of panic as he loomed over her. 'Just wait a minute…I'm not ready… Oh…'

'Really?'

'Oh,' she said again, this time more quietly and with wonder. How could she have forgotten how big he was in so short a time?

'There,' Lorenzo teased softly against her lips as he pressed her knees back. 'There, you see, you can… What a good, brave girl you are.'

'Yes, aren't I?' Carly agreed, groaning with satisfaction as he remained quite still, giving her every opportunity to savour the moment.

She grew bolder, and wrapped her ankles around his neck. He supported her, holding her bottom and kneading it gently as he sank slowly inside her. 'How does that feel?' he murmured, as if he didn't know.

It felt delicious. With Lorenzo nudging and rubbing places that only seemed more receptive to his touch now they had known it she could barely manage to voice a ragged sigh. He knew everything she liked as if by instinct. He took his time moving slowly, and even withdrawing completely, so that she knew the pleasure of having him re-enter her again and again and again, and he was right about them needing every inch of the bed. He was intent on working his way steadily through all the positions suggested by her ambitious doodles until he found the ones that pleased her most.

'You greedy girl,' he murmured softly, placing one finger over her swollen mouth.

'You make that sound like a compliment,' she whispered.

'That's because it was...'

Words dissolved into sensation as Lorenzo made lazy passes with his tongue against her lips. Then he plunged deep, matching that action with another, and repeating it until her hips moved convulsively beneath him. 'I want it... I want it again,' she panted in desperation.

'And you shall have it,' Lorenzo assured her. 'When I tell you to, you'll let go with me, and it will be bigger and fiercer and stronger and scarier than anything you've ever known.'

'I believe you,' she cried, beside herself with excitement.

She opened herself as wide as she could for him, holding herself in place, offering herself; wanting it, wanting him—

'Now!' he rasped fiercely in her ear, taking her with him

But this time he didn't stop when she quietened, but kept right on moving, slowly to begin with and then building the pace until they were working fiercely together. When the moment came it was like an explosion of pleasure, and when she cried out in amazement approaching fear he looked at her and knew he couldn't enjoy sex more than this. He needed this...

He needed her.

He shook himself round in time. What he needed was sex, pure and simple.

He needed Carly...

The words kept on like a siren call in his head. He drove it out and moved to take her again.

'Don't you ever need to rest?' she asked him.

'If you've had enough—'

'I didn't say that,' she assured him breathlessly, writhing sinuously on the bed. Putting her arms above her head, she allowed them to rest on the pillows in an attitude of wanton seduction. 'I just thought you might need to recharge your batteries.'

'I don't know which brand you use,' he said, progressing the metaphor, 'but I suggest you find yourself a more reliable supplier.'

'I think I just did.'

'Good...then why don't you shut up, relax, and let me do the work?'

That was the sort of instruction she was more than willing to take.

It was much, much later when Lorenzo suggested they take a shower together. 'And after that I suggest we indulge ourselves in a feast of chocolate and champagne.'

'I love your suggestions.'

He carried her into the bathroom and turned on the shower.

He didn't warn her about the icy water, and she shrieked as it cascaded over them.

'Not too cold for you, I hope?' Lorenzo queried dryly, and when she complained that it was he suggested a cure.

'You're insatiable,' she accused him.

'Aren't you glad?'

'I'm not complaining,' Carly assured him, 'merely offering an observation...' And now it was impossible to speak. Lorenzo had one arm braced against the wall, while the other held her bottom in place. The contrast between icy water and the heat inside her was incredible. 'You're amazing,' she groaned as he thrust into her.

'I can't fault your judgement,' he agreed.

'Shall we have macaroons in bed, as well as the champagne?' Lorenzo suggested when they were dry.

'When we've just had a shower?'

'Half the fun is getting dirty.'

'And the other half is getting clean?'

'You guessed it,' he said dryly with a grin.

He padded naked to the door, and as he turned back to her she thought again how beautiful he was.

'Or shall I just bring you chocolate and champagne?' he asked.

'You really do know the way to a woman's heart, Lorenzo.'

'As long as I can find my way to yours...'

Did he mean it? Carly turned her face into the pillow when Lorenzo left the room. Of course not! Words, like kisses, came so easily to him.

When he returned with a loaded tray she switched on her bright face. The truth was all that activity had given her quite an appetite. Lorenzo had brought champagne and chocolate as well as a plateful of dainty multicoloured macaroons.

'From Ladurée, the best tea shop in Paris,' he told her. 'I had them flown in especially for you.'

'Of course you did.'

'No, I really did,' he insisted, 'as a reward for arranging the party—and that was before I knew how good it was going to be. Now as this is something of an experiment for me I shall expect your full concentration...'

Carly tried to hide her smile as they gazed at each other, and failed. 'You've got it,' she said. Lorenzo could do that to you—however many times she warned herself to hold back on the emotion he could obliterate common sense with a look.

Carly soon discovered that one tiny chocolate macaroon could go a long way when it was crumbled. 'Oh, that's bad,' she gasped in the throes of recovery as Lorenzo finally came up for air. 'I'm going to make sure you go down for a very long time indeed.'

'I sincerely hope you do,' he said, smiling wickedly as he reached for another macaroon.

His good intentions were shot to hell, Lorenzo accepted as Carly lay sleeping in his arms. This was supposed to be emotion-free sex, no ties, no long-term repercussions for either of them. His judgement had always been flawless in the past, and now this! He wasn't sure he would ever be able to think straight again. The only thing he was sure about was no more female pupils *ever!* The best thing he could do was find an order of monks and hope they needed legal representation—

'Lorenzo...'

She'd sensed his restlessness and woken up. He sensed her need for reassurance. Kissing her, he brought her back into his arms. 'What is it, *cara mia?*' As he stared down into her trusting face he wanted to tell her everything he had decided, but how could he do that when it would shake the foundations of her life?

'What is it?' she said, sensing the shadow passing over him.

'Not now, baby…' Drawing her close, he kissed her again. Having seen her confidence blossom while they'd been together, he couldn't bring himself to destroy it now.

CHAPTER TWELVE

CARLY WENT INTO chambers early one morning the following week to clear up some papers before facing her final interview for the Unicorn scholarship that same afternoon. It was due to take place in front of a panel of senior lawyers chaired by Lorenzo. She hadn't really seen him since the night of the party but she felt confident, if anxious. She was going incommunicado until it was over, she decided, switching off her phone.

Now she wanted to be anywhere but here. She had never felt this apprehensive about an interview before, maybe because this time there had been vibes coming off Lorenzo, telling her however well prepared she was it wouldn't be straightforward.

She bodged the interview. And not just bodged it; by the time she left the room she was suffused in waves of uncertainty as to whether law was even the direction in which she wanted to go. Scrunching her mother's letter into a tiny ball, she braced herself to make the call.

What made it all the harder was that Lorenzo had let her down. He hadn't appeared on the panel. He hadn't even bothered to turn up and wish her luck. And okay, her phone was off, so he couldn't reach her that way, but surely he could have sent her a message somehow? She'd known all along her love affair with Lorenzo was one-sided: she was in love with Lorenzo; he was in love with sex. She'd had her eyes wide open from the start, but surely common human decency demanded some explanation for his absence?

Her mother picked up the phone, stemming her train of thought. She couldn't get a word in as her mother explained excitedly that everyone was waiting at the house for her news…

'I didn't get it—'

'Your father's poised to open the champagne—'

'Mum, please listen to me. Can't you tell him to hold the champagne?' Too late! She heard the cork pop. She waited for the cheers and the laughter to die down. 'Mum, I didn't get it…'

'What did you say?' Her mother's strangled whisper silenced the excited chatter in the background.

'I didn't get it,' Carly repeated dully, knowing how badly she'd let everyone down.

Her mother turned shrill as all the wasted dreams spilled out of her. 'How could it go so wrong?' she finished.

'It was my fault,' Carly confessed. 'I made a mess of the interview.'

'Is that all you have to say?' Her mother's voice had dropped to a driven whisper. 'Don't you care what this means to us?'

'I'm sorry… I don't know what else to say.'

'There must be a mistake,' her mother insisted, rallying. 'You'd never make a mess of the interview. You're overreacting, Carly. Why are you doing this to me?'

'I'm really sorry—can I speak to Dad?'

'You know what this is going to do to him, don't you? You read my letter, I hope! I told you about his stress levels—what do you think this is going to do to him?'

'Would it be better if I came home to break it to him myself?'

'No,' her mother shot back. 'I think you'd better stay away and lay low for a while until everything's died down.'

'Okay…' Carly bit down on her lip as the line went dead. Covering her head with her arms she let out a shuddering sigh. It was no use thinking the bottom had just fallen out of her world, even though it had; she had to pick herself up and carry on however much it hurt. And this time it really hurt. The panel had told her that her pupil master had absented himself from the panel.

Deserted a sinking ship, more like!

Lorenzo walked briskly round the luxury store with a personal shopper in tow. He knew how much winning the scholarship had meant to Carly and he was determined to soften the blow for her. He had resigned from the panel with immediate effect. He couldn't bring himself to endorse something that could never make her happy. At the end of the day he hadn't needed to say as much to the panel; they had come to the same conclusion he had—that her heart wasn't in it. She had talked a lot about her parents during her interview, apparently, but very little about herself. They assured him that although she was an outstanding candidate it wasn't what she really wanted in life, but she just hadn't seen that yet.

He'd seen her type before, Lorenzo reflected as he paid the bill and thanked the personal shopper—ambitious young lawyers on the threshold of life, following a route map laid out for them by their parents. Carly was so much more than that, she deserved so much more than that. He'd tried to ring her, but he could understand she must want some time alone.

The flat was empty when she got back. Louisa had already left for the Home Counties, and Lorenzo was…

Practically moved out!

Carly's stomach contracted painfully as she scanned his room again just to make sure. She knew his apartment was ready for him to move back into, but she hadn't realized he'd leave so abruptly—and so soon. She sat down on his bed to get over the shock of his desertion, but then she sprang up right away. She didn't want to touch, see or think about Lorenzo's bed. She didn't want to remember anything that had happened there.

The sound as she slammed the door echoed round the empty apartment, mocking her. Leaning back against a wall, she wrapped her arms around her waist and expelled a shuddering sigh. What a bright spark she'd turned out to be! She had slept with a man who held her fate in his hands, a man who didn't care, and now she'd lost the scholarship.

The scholarship… Closing her eyes as she thought about it, she relived the moment in the interview room when she had realised she didn't want it. What she had wanted was to please her parents. The scholarship meant nothing to her. What she wanted was Lorenzo and a working life where she could feel a real sense of achievement as she had after the Christmas party. Closing her eyes, she wished violently that Lorenzo were out of her head and she could identify the route she really wanted to take in life.

The clerks, the backroom boys at chambers who managed the barristers' diaries, had been kind to her when she had told them she'd flunked the interview. 'Why don't you plan some more parties?' they'd chorused. 'You're good at that.'

She had laughed with them, and then realised they were serious.

An event planner?

She shook her head, dismissing the idea at once. Her Northern night had been a one-off. Like Lorenzo.

And, like Lorenzo, never to be repeated, Carly told herself, switching on her phone.

She waited for it to initialise, and then saw that there were seven missed calls from Lorenzo. Frowning, she tried returning them, but he didn't pick up. Leave a message? She couldn't think of one—not one polite enough to write down, that was.

Determined to have it out with him face to face, she went to his new apartment where the smell of fresh paint caught her throat the moment the elevator doors opened. He hadn't been kidding about the flood; everything had been recently decorated. It must have been bad.

The elevator she'd travelled up in was private and reserved for the exclusive use of the owner of the penthouse in a prestigious block, one Lorenzo Domenico. It was all very impressive, even by Lorenzo's exacting standards. The concierge had greeted her in the lobby and had checked her credentials carefully before allowing her upstairs. Mr Domenico was out, he'd told her, but there was a mailbox outside his apartment in which she could leave her package of important documents.

Important documents? She had collected together as many A4 sheets of paper as she could find and had tied them ostentatiously with bright pink barristers' tape. The bundle was her passport up to Lorenzo's apartment, and nothing more. The hallway was impressive enough; Lorenzo's apartment, which took up most of the top floor overlooking London, must be sumptuous, Carly concluded, ringing the bell.

He wasn't in. She'd known that right away; his energy was missing.

She looked around as she waited, uncertain as to what to do next. For all its luxury the entrance to Lorenzo's palace lacked the patina of a home. It was just a new apartment in a new apartment block. There were no cooking aromas seeping under the door to suggest the gorgeous Italian-American who loved to cook, no scratches or stains, no finger smudges on the walls, everything was pristine, and completely soulless. Quite suddenly she missed the trappings of a home, somewhere filled with love and warmth. Love and warmth, she mused, those were the elusive magic ingredients, like the seasoning in Lorenzo's sauce. But perhaps this was enough for him, this gilded cage. Men measured success in terms of money and possessions, while women lusted after nests to feather, homes to clutter with memories…

Hefting the papers she'd brought with her into the waste shoot, she returned to Lorenzo's mailbox and posted the small gift-wrapped parcel she had bought for him before everything went wrong. She didn't want it hanging around and she couldn't bring herself to throw it away. It wasn't much in the monetary sense, even though she thought it special, and she would have bought her pupil master something for Christmas anyway, she had managed to persuade herself.

Lifting her chin, she started back to her flat. Bypassing the elevator she chose the stairs. Why hurry when she had almost two weeks to kill before the courts reconvened?

Lorenzo hit the button to the top floor. He considered an elevator essential. Shopping had to reach the penthouse somehow, and experience had taught him that if he didn't have a fast, reliable means of reaching the top floor, any grocery service he selected would complain.

The smell of newness hit him the moment he opened the front door. Tossing his jacket aside, he opened all the windows. He had thought about ordering flowers, and then realised it would have to wait until after Christmas. The best he could do for now was brew coffee and start cooking.

There was only one thing, one person, missing: his sparring partner, Carly Tate. He missed their verbal jousts as well as their tangles in the bedroom. But he wouldn't chase. He knew she'd probably be angry and she needed time to consider the suggestions he'd made in his letter. She might not take them well at first; she might not take them well ever, but he'd had to say what was on his mind.

She turned back when she was halfway home. She wasn't going to take this on the chin. She was fed up with doing that. Lorenzo couldn't just walk out on her. If she put this down to experience she would never forgive herself. She would sit on his doorstep if she had to and wait until he got back. A lack of self-confidence didn't mean you were a coward; it just meant you had to work harder at persuading yourself that a man hadn't bought you a fabulous dress as incentive to have sex with him.

And who needed an incentive to sleep with Lorenzo?

So had it been pay-off time?

No. Lorenzo had far more style than that.

Another woman, then? Madeline flashed into her mind.

The little green devils were always the hardest to deal with, but in all honesty she couldn't remember Lorenzo looking at Madeline that way. Maybe that was because she couldn't bear to think about him and Madeline after...

After what? Carly asked herself impatiently. Had there ever been anything between them except sex?

'Carly...' Madeline stood back in Lorenzo's hallway. 'This is a surprise!'

Not half as much for Madeline as it was for her, Carly thought angrily. Well, if she was about to make a bigger fool of herself than ever she might as well get on with it. 'Is he in?'

Waving a champagne flute, Madeline backed deeper into

Lorenzo's apartment. 'He's cooking in the kitchen. Shall I call him?'

Madeline was definitely weaving, Carly decided, narrowing her eyes. So they'd been drinking together. Everything inside her shrivelled into dust and then it exploded into cold, hard fury. Cooking was Lorenzo's preferred path to seduction; he'd made no secret of it. She should have known he wouldn't be without a bed-mate for long. And Madeline was the perfect choice—another lawyer, glamorous, clever, witty, and even now, slightly drunk, she looked amazing.

Absolutely amazing.

While she looked a fright, Carly realised, feeling her spirit drain away as she caught sight of herself in a mirror. She had really outdone herself today. She was wearing the usual thrift-shop suit, and now she saw she'd spilled something down it. And she'd gone into the interview looking like that? She grimaced. It was so humiliating. Nothing, *nothing* could be worse than this—

'I got the scholarship,' Madeline announced. 'Did you hear?'

'You…' Pressing her lips together, Carly made her head move up and down. 'That's such great news. I'm really pleased for you.' And she was, strangely, but her nose was stinging, really hurting, in the way noses did when tears were threatening.

She took the opportunity to escape when Madeline turned around to call Lorenzo from the kitchen. She didn't need anyone to explain to her what was happening here, though as she fled she heard Lorenzo say something she didn't catch. She did hear Madeline's reply.

'Oh, it was nothing important, and they've gone now…'

Make that no one important, and Madeline had got it right, Carly thought, clutching the cold stone handrail on the bridge.

The river Thames was moving slowly to the sea, a dull, grey dish-rag of a river, reflecting a sullen sky. It perfectly mirrored her mood. She was transfixed by the rolling water, and by the tears dripping off the end of her nose into it. She could see now that she had been too complacent about everything; too naïve, too fat—

'Carly?'

'Lorenzo!' She bridled and backed away. 'What are you doing here?'

'Is this your private bridge?'

She glared at him.

'What are you doing here, Carly? Not planning a swim, I hope?'

Emotions churned inside her as she looked at him. She wanted to kill him. She wanted to launch herself into his arms... And kill him.

'I saw you from the window. I couldn't believe it was you. Where on earth have you been?'

'Where have *I* been?' Anger ripped through her, made all the more intense by the realisation that she had gone to pieces right under his balcony—she couldn't even get that right.

'You're coming with me,' he said. 'You look frozen.'

He was right about one thing: she was ice inside, and not about to thaw any time soon. 'I'm not coming back with you.' Not while Madeline was there!

'Did I say you had a choice?'

And have Madeline stare at her pityingly the whole time? It just wasn't going to happen. 'Lorenzo! Let go of me.'

'I have a sauce on the go, and woe betide you if it burns.'

She struggled furiously, and then stopped. If she went with him she could have her say, and, Madeline or no Madeline, she was going to let him have it with both barrels.

CHAPTER THIRTEEN

STANDING WITH HIS pleasure-giving hands planted on his ecstasy-dealing hips, Lorenzo glanced round his new apartment with pride. 'Well,' he said to Carly. 'What do you think?'

What did she think? She could smell Madeline's perfume! Still tender from his incredible love-making, she was still stinging from his vanishing act, and on the edge of rage. What threw her a little was the warmth and enthusiasm in Lorenzo's eyes where she failed to detect the slightest hint of guilt. She glanced round suspiciously. The apartment was even more magnificent than she had imagined, with stripped pine floors, cream walls, and splashes of colour provided by well-chosen modern art. There was a state-of-the-art sound system in one corner, and all the other technical gizmos she might have expected a man like Lorenzo to own. All in all it was fabulous: light, airy, and mostly open plan—so little chance for anyone to hide.

'What?' Lorenzo said, watching her.

'Where's your friend?' Carly tipped her chin at an aggressive angle.

'My friend?' Lorenzo paused for a moment and then enlightenment struck him. 'You mean Madeline?'

'This isn't funny, Lorenzo,' Carly snapped, seeing the suspicion of a smile hovering round his mouth. 'Where is she? In your bed?'

This was answered with a quizzical look. Refusing to be deterred, she set off on her hunt. Flinging open the first door, she peered inside. The bedroom was immaculate, and looked as if it had been put together by an interior designer. She couldn't imagine Lorenzo arranging the fabulous buttermilk suede cushions with such precision. Behind the next door she found a broom cupboard. Slamming it, she wheeled around.

'Why do I get the feeling you're not happy with me?' Lorenzo said.

He looked so gorgeous standing there she almost relented. Almost. 'Why do *I* get the feeling your sauce is burning?'

'What?' He whirled around and rushed to pull the pan off the cooker, shaking his hand and cursing after he did so.

'Too hot for you, Lorenzo?' Carly demanded pointedly.

Turning to face her, he granted her an ironic look.

Behind the next door she found the most sumptuous bathroom she had ever seen…all marble and glass with steel fittings and a bath big enough for two…

'I'd happily show you round,' Lorenzo offered.

She paused with her hand on the next door handle.

'Just a thought,' he murmured. 'Oh, and by the way, are you staying for supper?'

'You've got a nerve,' Carly said, turning. Her throat dried. If only she'd had some mental armour to deal with the way her body responded to Lorenzo. He was standing in the open-plan kitchen with his hands on his hips, looking magnificent. His jeans moulded every inch of his impressive lower body, and with such brazen accuracy her cheeks burned. His sleeves were rolled up, revealing the muscles on his arms. He was seriously good-looking, as well as a serious distraction.

Carly dragged her thoughts back to the reason for her

visit. 'Where were you today?' Disappointment and distress rang in her voice, but it was too late to stop now. 'Were you too busy coaching Madeline on scholarship technique to have time for me? I bet you found time to attend her interview—'

'Are you jealous of Madeline?'

'Don't be so ridiculous! And don't you dare try to turn this round on me. You should have been there. You're the chairman of the scholarship committee, and my pupil master—'

'Which is a good enough reason for me to step out, don't you think?' Lorenzo cut in calmly.

'No, I don't!' But even as she raged at him her sensible self insisted he was right. She shook her head and when she spoke again her voice was husky. 'If you felt that our relationship affected things why didn't you warn me sooner?'

'Because you were incommunicado,' Lorenzo reminded her. 'Because no one knew where you were.'

'But didn't you think I'd want to see you before I went in?' As her voice broke she turned away.

'I've had enough of this,' Lorenzo said. Crossing the room, he seized hold of her. 'Look at me, Carly…'

He had never wanted to kiss a woman so much in his life. When Carly was aroused she was magnificent. Her cheeks were flushed, her lips were crimson, and the tip of her nose with its sprinkling of freckles had turned white in her fury. Her wild Celtic hair rose above her shoulders like an inferno painted in red and gold, and yet coppery baby fronds were pressed to her brow. It was more than humankind, or at least he, could withstand—

'Get off me, Lorenzo, I'm warning you!'

Her slap began at her knees, and travelled like a comet to his chin, by which time her tiny hand had turned into a fist. He blessed his lightning reflexes. Catching hold of her wrist just as her hand connected with his face, he snatched her other wrist too, just to be on the safe side. But then he found it impossible to stop laughing, which on reflection was a mistake. She had taken some of his fashion advice on board, including how good she looked in stiletto heels. He cursed violently when she stamped down hard on his toe. 'God save me from women and from redheads in particular! You don't need a mentor, you need a keeper with a whip—'

But their struggles were too enjoyable to come even close to anger, and she writhed against him, making the little sounds of frustration he knew so well, he could only thank God she'd found emotion, and wasn't afraid of showing it. He guessed she had spent her whole life listening to other people emote while she got on quietly with her work. Maybe his family went too far the other way, but at least they had never been afraid of expressing their feelings. When he let her go she said, 'I'm sorry… I don't know what came over me—'

'Passion,' he suggested. 'Maybe that came over you. Anyway, forget it.'

Forget it while Lorenzo stood nursing his chin? She was mortified and ashamed of herself. She had never resorted to violence, and never would again. But he was right; there was a lot bottled up inside her, and she hadn't even realised how much up to now. That was one thing Lorenzo understood about her; he knew how to free the stopper that kept all the feelings in.

She looked at him. They had invoked a world of passion; an electric storm of passion. She had always believed herself to be one of the dullest people alive, but that was before she started seeing herself through Lorenzo's eyes. Maybe there was hope for her after all…

'Madeline's not here,' Lorenzo confirmed. 'She came

round to share her news, and I opened a bottle of champagne. It seemed the decent thing to do. Then she left. She was already pretty merry by the time she arrived.'

It made sense, Carly admitted to herself. Her gaze strayed, as it always did, to Lorenzo's socks: the barometer of his mood. They were green, with angry red polka dots, which couldn't have been more appropriate for the way she was feeling, for a change.

'You haven't read my letter, have you?' he said.

'Your letter?' She looked up.

'You didn't go back and check your cubby-hole after the interview?'

She gave a shrug. 'I didn't exactly feel like hanging around.'

'But you collected up your stuff.' He glanced at the heap of things she'd brought with her from chambers.

'Of course I did. It's the Christmas recess. But I didn't look at it. The clerks packed it all up for me—'

'So you don't know that I've resigned from the scholarship committee?'

'What?' she said softly. 'Why would you do that?'

'Don't you know?'

Everything went very still. 'No…'

'Because you're more important to me than any seat on a board. Don't ask me why,' he added dryly before she could go starry-eyed.

'What exactly are you saying, Lorenzo?'

'I got out before the scandal broke.'

'What scandal?'

'This one.' He dragged her close. 'I'm not so sure there would have been a scandal,' he said, looking down at her, 'but I wasn't taking any chances, and it's you I care about. You and your future, Carly Tate. I want what's right for you—'

'And you think you're going to determine my future now?'

With an angry cry she pushed him away. She'd had enough of people deciding what she should do. But when Lorenzo looked at her as if to say it was her decision—her life, her career, something only she must decide—her pummelling fists softened to searching hands, and a jolt of pure longing drew a sound from her throat.

He brought her back into his arms then and held her firmly the way she liked. His lips were cunning as they prepared the way for his tongue, and the intrusion, the sudden penetration, the taste, the strength and the scent of him all combined as they always did to steal her strength away. Lucky for her he was so strong. He took her weight easily with the smallest adjustment of his powerful frame, and all the while he kept on kissing her deeply and intimately, until her nipples grew painfully tender again, and she was drowning in waves of needing him.

'*Santo Dio!* I've missed you,' he murmured.

Should she swim against the tide of arousal, or should she sink beneath it and drown? 'Just don't treat me like a child, Lorenzo. You can't pick me up and put me down again when it suits you.'

'Who said anything about putting you down?'

'I needed you, Lorenzo. I needed your support—'

'I was moving into my new apartment. I left you a letter to explain…' He sighed. 'And I was shopping.'

'Shopping?' Now she was incensed.

'Christmas?' he reminded her. 'I thought you would have read about my decision regarding the committee. I thought you needed time. I guessed you would be going home to your family for Christmas.'

That clearly wasn't on the cards, he guessed, judging by the look on her face, but as he reached out to her she thrust him away again. 'What am I going to do with you?' he demanded with frustration. They were facing each other like warring tigers. He hadn't felt this way since…ever, he guessed.

'Next time you kiss a woman, kiss her because you mean it, Lorenzo! Because you want to! Because you can't stop yourself.'

The irony wasn't lost on him. He had never wanted to kiss a woman more, but he blamed himself for upsetting her even though he suspected he wasn't aware of the cause of half of it. There was so much going on inside her head he didn't know about. 'Why don't you tell me what's really upset you?'

'You…and other things.' She gave him a cold stare that warned of her feelings switching off.

With a sound of frustration he jutted out his chin. 'Okay, if it makes you feel better, punch me. Go on,' he urged, angling his head to make it easy for her. 'Why hold back now?'

She stared at him tensely for a moment, and then she made a little noise—not quite a laugh, but getting there.

'You're impossible!' she flung at him, shaking her head.

'And you're perfectly reasonable,' he said back. 'Now let's get real. I've got a bottle of Krug open waiting for someone to take a slug out of it. Interested?'

She hesitated and then followed him as he turned to the kitchen.

Climbing up on one of the bar stools, she waited in silence while he found some glasses and poured the champagne. 'Cheers!' he said softly, clinking glasses with her.

'Happy Christmas, Lorenzo…' She wouldn't look at him.

'So, what plans have you made?' he prompted.

Thanks to the revolving chairs and the way she'd angled herself he couldn't see her face, but then he saw her shoulders shaking and swung her round. He stopped her sobbing the only way he knew, with a kiss, and with his arms binding her close so she would know how it felt to be safe. 'You taste salty,' he said, pulling back so he could smile against her mouth.

'So do you,' she said with a little laugh that made his heart swell.

'Well, are you going to tell me what's wrong, or not?' He tipped her chin, giving her nowhere to look but in his eyes.

'My mother doesn't want me home.' She tossed the words off as if they were of no importance to her; she even managed the approximation of a smile.

'She doesn't want you home?' he repeated incredulously.

'That's right. She said it would be better if I left things to calm down a bit after the scholarship fiasco.'

He was raging inside. What sort of family made a child feel that it couldn't come home unless it brought a prize? It put a price on love, and it seemed to him Carly could never meet that price however hard she worked.

'I didn't think it would hurt so much,' she admitted with a frankness that brought them closer.

Lifting her face, she stared him right in the eyes as if to say she was all right now. He didn't believe her for a minute. 'So, what shall we do about it?' he said.

'We?'

'Well, *I* don't want to be on my own for Christmas.' He had meant to make it easier for her, but the last thing he wanted happened—more tears, and this time they were tears of humiliation.

'You don't have to be kind to me, Lorenzo.'

'Kind?' He gave her one of his looks. 'Me?'

'Stop it. You know what I mean. I'll be fine—'

'I don't *have* to do anything, but if I want to…'

Lorenzo would do exactly as he pleased, Carly thought, silently finishing the sentence for him. But she didn't want to be anyone's charity case, and she wasn't sure how long she could keep this up, this casual pretence that sex was fun, kissing was fun, eating together was fun, when there was so much love inside her scorching a trail for him through her heart.

CHAPTER FOURTEEN

'I'VE COME TO a decision,' Carly told Lorenzo. 'I'd like to be alone for a few days. I need to sort out my head. I need to learn how to stand on my own two feet.'

'You've been doing that all your life, as far as I can tell. You're strong, Carly. Why can't you see that?'

'I'll admit to being determined and driven, but I've always walked in the direction someone else has pointed me. What I want now is time to work out where I want to go.'

'You'd consider quitting law?' His eyes narrowed. He wasn't going to tell her what to do, though it was so obvious, at least to him. The last thing she needed was someone else pulling her strings.

'I haven't made any decisions yet. I thought the scholarship was what I wanted, and that it would be an end in itself, but I was wrong, and now I need a new goal.'

'How about personal happiness?' he suggested. He was growing impatient with her inability to see how easy it was to throw a life away on someone else's aspirations. 'Your parents will get over this—'

'You don't know them.'

And, increasingly, he didn't want to. 'You'll do lots of things to make them proud.'

'I understand why they're disappointed,' she said. 'They gave up so much for me. They're entitled—'

'Parents aren't entitled to live their children's lives for them,' he cut across her. 'They can only love them, and equip them for the world as best they can—'

'That's your way of thinking, Lorenzo, not mine—'

'But it's your life—'

'And I'm not sure what my life is right now, so please—'

'I won't stop you going,' he said as she glanced towards the door. He eased away from the cabinets to let her get by him. 'If you need me you know where I am.'

An expression crossed her face that told him she was surprised and hurt he could just back off like that. His intention had been to give her space, but maybe space wasn't what she needed.

'Enjoy your supper,' she said.

It was a crossroads, a turning point in his life. She let herself out of the front door while the energy they had created was still springing round him. He wasn't about to wait around for it to fade. Snatching up his jacket, he went after her.

The moment she opened the front door of her flat he knew she'd been crying. 'Go wash your face. I'm taking you out,' he said.

She stared at him blankly, and then to his absolute relief she opened the door fully, murmuring, 'Come in…'

He wanted to take her in his arms straight away. She was so vulnerable, he would do anything to heal the hurt inside her, but he held back, respecting her desire to find the path she wanted by herself.

Thankfully, she rallied quickly, the way he'd hoped she would. 'Where are you taking me?' she said after a protracted tidying-up session in her bedroom.

'That's my surprise.'

'But it's Christmas Eve,' she reminded him. 'Won't everywhere be too busy for us to find a table?'

'It will be fine,' he reassured her. 'Trust me.'

She gave him an ironic look. 'You'd better tell me if I'm dressed appropriately?'

If she'd been wearing a dustbin liner tied with string she'd have looked just as beautiful to him.

'No comment?' She gave a twirl.

The ice-blue sweater against her ivory skin made her look ethereal, beautiful. He had only one suggestion. 'Let your hair down…'

Reaching up, she removed the tortoiseshell pin holding it, and the whole glittering cascade fell and bounced around her shoulders.

'Perfect. Do you have a warm jacket?'

'How warm do I need to be?'

'No clues,' he said. 'You're too good a lawyer. If I'm not careful you'll have the whole story out of me before I'm ready for you to know.'

The smile on her face was the only reward he wanted.

Her face turned ashen when she realised where they were going.

'You said nothing when I asked if you trusted me,' he reminded her.

'Yes, I know, but I *hate* flying.'

'I'll ask you again—do you trust me?'

She gulped and stared up the steps of the small aeroplane. 'Are you the pilot?'

He laughed. 'Unless you'd like to take a turn?'

'No! I just—'

'What you'll just do,' he said, 'is sit in a very comfortable seat, reading a selection of magazines, while sipping champagne and nibbling some delicious snacks.'

'I will?' she said uncertainly.

'You will.'

'Will it be a long fright…flight?'

'Quite a short one, actually,' he soothed, escorting her up the steps. 'And now, if you will excuse me, I have a plane to fly…'

Lorenzo must be taking her to Italy, Carly guessed as they took off. She knew he had family there. Or perhaps a Christmas ski trip. But if that were true, why hadn't he suggested she pack even warmer clothes?

It was no use worrying about it now she was buckled into her seat. She just had to accept they were heading somewhere—

And landing already?

Not Italy, then.

So where?

Peering out of the window told her nothing. One runway looked much like another in the dark.

'Did you enjoy the flight?' Lorenzo said, ducking his head as he came back into the cabin to collect her. 'I told you it wouldn't be long.'

'So where are we?'

'That's my surprise.'

As they stepped outside the aircraft and the sleet hit her in the face she read the sign.

'I told you it would be a surprise, didn't I?'

But not a good one, Carly thought in silence.

Linking arms with her, Lorenzo hurried her across the tarmac towards a waiting limousine. 'I'm taking you home,' he said as if that should please her. 'Families should be together at Christmas. It's a time for reconciliation, and for love…'

It wasn't much of a village, though she was right; it was in the middle of nowhere. He wasn't sure what he'd been expecting, but this wasn't it. Carly's talk of an English village had conjured up an impression in his head of a picture-perfect place like something you might find on the front of a greeting card. This was more like a village some local planning team had come up with fast on a Friday afternoon. It had been built without thought for the eventual inhabitants' convenience, either side of a busy main road. He could see why Carly would want to escape; it was harder to understand why anyone would want to settle there in the first place.

He turned to smile reassurance at her, having noticed how quiet she had become. He had hoped this trip back home would give him the answers she wouldn't, but now he was beginning to wish he'd had more patience and had waited until she was ready to tell him.

When the limousine had halted he helped her out. He was using a driver because he had wanted to sit with her, but she'd put acres between them on the back seat. She was going home, he thought, frowning inwardly. Shouldn't that have been a cause for celebration? Maybe those answers he was looking for were right here.

He stood close to her as she rang the front door bell. She had nodded when he had asked her if she was okay, but the set of her shoulders told him something different. He wanted to tell her it would be fine, and that he was there for her, but suddenly even he wasn't so sure he could make it right. For a start, it was up to Carly to decide how much or how little she wanted to tell her parents about them…

The door was opened by a thin, pinched-face woman who looked as if she sucked lemons for a treat.

'Mum!'

The excitement in Carly's voice contrasted starkly with the way the older woman flinched.

'Mrs Tate,' he said, extending his hand formally. His hope

had been to distract Carly so she wouldn't notice her mother's reaction to her. The calculation in Mrs Tate's eyes as she turned her attention to him was a real eye-opener.

'This is Lorenzo, Mother,' Carly said, blissfully unaware, he sincerely hoped, of the undercurrents running from the house to the step. 'Lorenzo Domenico…my pupil master in chambers?'

Mrs Tate stood back to take a proper look at him. 'To what do we owe this honour?' she said.

'Can we come in?' Carly prompted with an edge of anxiety in her voice.

'Of course you can,' her mother said, standing back. 'What are you waiting for?'

A welcome, maybe, he thought.

Once inside they walked down a narrow hallway and into an impressively neat sitting room. An older man was sitting in an easy chair watching football on the television. He looked weary, and barely glanced up, though judging by his slippers he had little enough cause for exhaustion.

'Mr Tate?' It was a relief when the man turned to look at him, and even more of a relief to see his gaze brighten.

'Yes, that's me,' he said, a little awkwardly, as if he were unused to being in the spotlight. Then his face transformed, and he sprang up. 'Carly!' he said, going to her.

'Dad!'

It was touching to see them embrace; it brought some warmth into the chilly atmosphere.

'You've put on weight, Carly.' Her mother's voice shattered the touching tableau. 'You need to watch that,' she said.

Carly's cheeks reddened, and her father returned mildly to his seat.

'My other daughter will be back soon.'

He realised Mrs Tate was addressing him, and speaking as if she expected him to be riveted by this piece of information.

'Olivia,' she prompted, as if news of her younger daughter had travelled far and wide. 'The beautiful sister,' she added, in case he was in any doubt.

'Oh?' He smiled pleasantly, after shooting a glance at Carly. He had to remember they were discussing her sister, but in his opinion there was no one more beautiful than Carly.

Olivia chose that very moment to breeze in, in a flurry of cold air and childish perfume.

'Carly!' she exclaimed as if all her Christmases had come at once. Ignoring everyone else in the room, Olivia threw her arms around her sister and danced about with her. She was deaf to her mother's pleading that if she didn't stop she might break something.

From what he could see there was already a litter of broken hearts in the room.

'Carly, come with me.'

His jaw worked with annoyance as her mother uttered this instruction. She had broken father and daughter apart, and now she was doing the same to her two daughters. What was wrong with the woman? He held back from comment; his up-bringing wouldn't allow him to countermand an instruction from Carly's mother in her own home. He would just have to fix the damage later.

'Are you pregnant?'

Carly's eyes widened. Her mother had barricaded them in the tiny kitchen, and now she stood barring the only escape route with her back firmly planted against the door.

'Why do you ask?' If she was pregnant, she would need her mother's support, surely?

'Because I can't think of a single reason why a man like

that pupil master of yours would fly you up here in a private
jet just to see us.' Her mother's thin lips pursed as she waited
for a response.

'He said it was Christmas, a time for families to be together.'

'That's never bothered you in the past.'

'I only ever missed one Christmas at home, and that was
when I was on a gap year from university—'

'But you didn't fly back then, did you?'

'You know I didn't. I was in India. I'm sorry. I didn't
realise…I should have been here—'

'Yes, you should,' her mother said impatiently, frowning.
'So *are* you pregnant?'

She had been brought up to tell the truth, and everyone
knew condoms failed, and people got pregnant all the time.
'I don't know…' Carly met her mother's cold gaze steadily.
They could both hear Lorenzo, his deep voice providing a
melodious counterpoint to Olivia's delighted laughter.

'Well,' her mother said with a knowing air. 'You needn't
think a man like that's going to marry you…' Glancing
towards the door, she made it clear whom she considered the
more suitable candidate to be. 'If he has got you pregnant the
best you can hope for is a pay-off. Any mistress to a man like
that would have to be—'

'Beautiful, Mother?' Carly cut in. 'Stylish? Content to live
in the lap of luxury provided by Lorenzo? We both know I
don't fit any of those categories, don't we?'

'Don't turn your bitterness and disappointment on me,' her
mother shot back. 'If you're pregnant, have an abortion.'

The moment's silence rang on and on.

'Don't look so scandalised,' Carly's mother insisted.
'You've always been the practical member of the family. If
there's a problem there's a solution—wasn't that what you
always used to say to me?'

Carly flinched. She hadn't realised that so much bitterness had built up over the years. It might be too late, but she had to try one last time. 'You gave up so much for me.'

'Yes, I did,' her mother said. 'But that's behind us now.'

Was it? Would it ever be behind them? No, Carly thought, it was here with them now in the tiny kitchen like a malign force—every penny spent, every missed hair appointment that had gone to provide for some expensive textbook. And she hadn't seen it. Had she been too self-absorbed to see it? She had—and this was the price she had to pay. 'If I am pregnant you wouldn't really want me to abort your grandchild, would you?' Her throat constricted as she waited for her mother to answer.

'Make up your own mind,' her mother said dismissively. 'You never listen to me anyway. I just hope you're not on your way to making a bigger fool of yourself than usual.'

As Lorenzo's laughter sounded from the other room Mrs Tate moved away from the door. 'You'd better go back in if you're to have the slightest hope of hanging on to him.'

Blinded by tears, Carly blundered through the door.

'Carly…'

Lorenzo got to his feet the moment she entered the room. He was smiling, and there was such a change in the atmosphere after the frost in the kitchen it took her a moment to adapt. The small sitting room was unusually full of life. Her father had even switched off the television. But as Lorenzo stepped forward to take hold of her hands she got the horrible feeling he was about to make an announcement. She was so disorientated and distressed after the talk with her mother she managed to persuade herself that Lorenzo wanted to comfort her when he explained that he was going to marry her sister. It was the only thing that made sense; they were both so beautiful. She could even hear him saying it: 'Mr and Mrs

Tate, I have been struck by a thunderbolt and have no alternative other than to ask for the hand of your daughter Olivia—'

'Carly?' Lorenzo said, dipping his head to stare her in the eyes. 'Where are you now?'

In the middle of a nightmare. Blinking, she refocused. Her mother and father had returned to their usual places either side of the fire. Her mother sat on the edge of her easy chair, while her father sat well back, as if bracing himself for confrontation. Olivia sat in silence on the sofa staring up at her.

For the first time in her life she couldn't bring herself to meet her sister's gaze. This time it wasn't a question of yielding a favourite toy, or the last chocolate in the box, it was the threat of losing the man she loved.

The man at the centre of the drama stood in front of her, making the tiny sitting room seem claustrophobic. Whatever had happened, whatever misunderstandings there had been between them, Lorenzo was the only person who made sense of her life. He was the direction she wanted to take; she just hadn't realised it before. And now it was too late.

CHAPTER FIFTEEN

'CARLY'S OVERWHELMED at returning home,' Lorenzo said to explain her silence. 'I'm glad you two had time together,' he told her mother, but something in his eyes left Mrs Tate in no doubt that he knew what she had done.

The tension that followed was suddenly too much for Carly, and she bolted for the stairs. She was halfway up them before she remembered she didn't have a room in the house any longer. Fortunately, Olivia was right behind her.

'My room,' Livvie said. 'Left at the top of the stairs.'

'My old room…' Carly smiled as she looked around. Plain fabrics had been replaced by chintz, and there was lace at the window.

'It's a bit frilly for you,' Livvie said, reading her sister's thoughts. 'I hope you don't object to my taking it over, only it was bigger than mine. You don't mind, do you, Carly?'

'No, of course I don't mind. You get the rooftops…' Carly turned to stare out of the window at a view she knew so well. She used to imagine all the hidden miles rolling back behind the chimney pots…

'I thought I'd better take the bigger room since it looks like I'm stuck here for life.'

Carly turned to look at her sister. Olivia had flopped down

on the bed. 'You're not stuck here any more than I was. Not unless you want to be, Livvie.'

'I've missed you…' Livvie patted the bed by her side.

'And I've missed you…' They hugged.

'So, is this Lorenzo special?'

There could be no secrets between sisters as close as they were, Carly realised. 'Lorenzo?' She gave a dry laugh. 'Anyone can see Lorenzo's special—far too special for me.'

'No one's too special for you,' Livvie argued hotly. 'And why would he bring you all this way if he didn't care for you?'

'His good deed for the year, maybe.'

'Carly, what's happened to you? You never used to be so cynical.'

'I never used to be much of anything, unless being a bookworm counts—'

'That's not true!' Livvie exclaimed with exasperation. 'You've always been the most wonderful sister to me. You're kind and loyal and brave. And you had the courage to escape.'

'You have that same courage. We're sisters. We're out of the same egg.'

'The same bitter old husk, don't you mean?'

'Livvie… Don't say that about Mother. She's done her best. But it's never enough, can't you see? She never quite managed to catch up with those wealthy friends of hers.'

'Then she should get herself some real friends,' Olivia argued fiercely.

By the time the two girls returned to the sitting room Lorenzo seemed to have worked magic. He had certainly put their parents at ease.

The atmosphere could hardly remain tense while Lorenzo was around, Carly reflected, but she wasn't ready for her mother's next remark.

'Why don't you stay over?' her mother invited. 'We've got two spare rooms now Carly's gone. Of course,' she hurried to explain, 'Christmas Day is a simple affair in the Tate household, and not up to your usual standards—just lunch at the golf club, followed by a few drinks. If I make a call now I'm sure they'll put on a couple of extra places.' Her eyes were already gleaming at the thought of introducing Lorenzo round.

'How kind of you, Mrs Tate,' Lorenzo said politely. 'I'd love nothing more, but I must admit I've made other plans for your daughter.'

As her mother tensed Carly felt sure the whole world was holding a collective breath.

'Are you ready, Carly?' he said, turning to her.

Why had she ever doubted him? Why had she ever doubted Livvie? Throwing her arms around Livvie's neck, she hugged her tight, begging her softly, 'Come and see me soon.'

'I will,' Livvie assured her in the same passionate undertone.

Lorenzo was quiet on the drive back to the airport and Carly's cheeks were burning as she imagined what he must be thinking. Her family home was shabby and parochial in comparison to his elegant city centre penthouse. She'd never seen her childhood home through a visitor's eyes before, never felt the tensions that existed between her mother and father to this extent.

The saddest thing was that she could remember a time when love was king, and possessions, like people's position in life, took second place. But that had been a long time ago, and seemed now almost like a dream that had never existed outside her imagination.

He was quiet because he was thinking about the suburban house they'd just left. In so many respects it was superior to the chaotic family home where he'd been brought up, but in the ways that mattered Carly's family home was impoverished. There were many more ways that cruelty could be dealt than in a blow, and Carly had done well to get away and forge a life for herself. He was so proud of her; her strength of character shone through everything he'd seen today.

'Lorenzo, I'm so sorry—'

'Sorry? For what?'

'I would have thought that was obvious.' She met his gaze fearlessly as she always did.

'Not to me.' He squeezed her hand.

'You don't have to be kind,' she insisted, pulling away. 'I know what you were trying to do back there.'

'Do you?' He smiled as he saw her cheeks pink up. 'You have no idea,' he assured her. Dragging her close, he brushed the tears from her cheeks with his thumb pads and then he kissed her and kept on kissing her until she believed him.

It was too late and too stormy to fly back to London, and so Lorenzo asked the chauffeur to take them to the nearest luxury hotel that had a room to spare.

'On Christmas Eve in Manchester?' Carly said, turning to look at him in surprise.

Her eyes were tear-stained and he knew she was still hurting. The damage her mother had done wasn't something that could be eradicated in a few hours; it would take a lot more time than that. Frustration was gnawing away inside him because he'd failed to shield her from the hurt. He wanted to reach inside her and wrench it out. He wanted to take her in his arms and reassure her and kiss that look off her face. He wanted to hold her hand and take her into a park where they could fool around and feed the ducks, and she would laugh. She didn't laugh much, and now he knew why.

'So what did you think of my family?' she asked him.

'I liked your sister.' He smiled as he spoke. What was not to like? Livvie was childlike and eager to please, and almost as wounded as Carly in her way.

'She's very pretty, isn't she?'

His brows drew together as he thought about it. Olivia was certainly a pleasure to look at in the same way he might enjoy looking at an interesting work of art, but did she move him? Did she make him feel like Carly made him feel? Not in a million years. He felt warm towards Olivia because of the way Olivia felt about her sister, and that was it. 'She's not as beautiful as you,' he said, holding Carly's gaze. And then he kissed her. She made him feel so good. She was beautiful inside and out. Maybe Olivia was too, but he had no interest in finding out. He'd found the woman he wanted.

'And my father?'

'Henpecked,' he said bluntly, pulling back to answer her as she deserved. 'Though an interesting man with an interesting story to tell about his life and his hobbies.'

'Do you really think so?' She looked astounded.

'Yes, I do. Did you know, for instance, that he builds model airplanes in his shed?'

'No,' Carly said with amazement. 'I only hope mother doesn't put a stop to it. I can't imagine she'd like all that dust and glue flying about—'

'Talking of flying,' he interrupted, 'I've promised to take your father up with me one day.' As he spoke his jaw firmed in a way that told her he would do that regardless of what anyone else thought about the idea.

'And my mother?' she asked him softly, staring down at her hands.

'Your mother is tense and anxious like a lot of people are

when they encounter something new, or something beyond their control.'

She seemed relieved he hadn't gone on the attack. 'Taking my father flying is certainly that!'

'She loves him in her way, and I think she'll worry about him in the same way she worries about you.'

She made a dismissive sound at that. 'Don't get carried away, Lorenzo. I know you're good with words, but we're not in court now. I don't mind. You can tell me exactly what you think.'

But she would mind. Whatever Mrs Tate was like she was Carly's mother. 'Your mother might relax more if she trusted her children to get on with their lives,' he said carefully. 'She doesn't need to find a husband for Olivia or a career for you. You're both capable of doing that for yourselves.'

'Do you think Olivia should have a husband?'

There was an edge in her voice.

'It's up to Olivia. I think she should start by finding some work outside the home she cares about, and then she would feel liberated.'

'And me?'

'A home life outside your work?' he suggested dryly.

'How profound you've become, Signor Domenico,' she mocked him.

'Carly, I haven't changed.' He touched her hand. 'And now...I think we've arrived.' He gazed out of the tinted window as the limousine slowed to a halt.

As Lorenzo came round to her side of the car Carly couldn't help wondering how far he would go to give all those things he'd talked about for Olivia and for her a helping hand. She pushed her concerns to one side as he gave the driver a generous tip and then asked the man to pick them up early the next morning.

'Early?' The word slipped out before she could stop herself.

'Was that a complaint?' Lorenzo challenged softly, taking hold of her hand.

'Lorenzo, this is fabulous…'

He had brought her to an exquisitely restored Georgian manor house deep in the Cheshire countryside. It was an award-winning hotel, Carly learned from reading one of their embossed cards while Lorenzo checked them in. The village was choco-late-box picture-perfect, the house lovely, and their welcome warm and unpretentious. It was very Lorenzo, she concluded.

'Only the best is good enough for you, *bella signorina,*' he said, gesturing towards the staircase.

The best turned out to be a sumptuous suite with a vast four-poster bed in the centre of the bedroom. The bed was dressed with ivory silk, and there was every conceivable aid to comfort in the room. There was also a space-age bathroom down the tiny hallway full of luxury products that could easily tempt you to stay for ever, and a small sitting room with an elegant dining room off. 'You really didn't have to go to all this expense,' Carly exclaimed as she gazed around. 'But I'm glad you did,' she added mischievously.

He started to laugh. Nothing made him happier than seeing Carly smile. As he watched she tried out the mattress, bounc-ing on it. He'd restrained himself long enough. Dropping down beside her, he brought her into his arms. She tasted wonderful; her skin was soft and fragrant like a peach, and he was ravenous for fruit…

'We're wearing far too many clothes,' she pointed out sensibly.

'I couldn't agree more.' His face was close to hers and he smiled against the plump, yielding cushion of her lips. 'But there's one thing I want you to do first…'

She yelped in disappointment as he moved away. 'What?'

she said, running her hand down his back in a way that was guaranteed to change his mind if he didn't move fast. 'My letter,' he reminded her. 'Did you bring it with you?'

The erotic mist slowly lifted from her eyes. She'd searched for the letter after he'd told her about it, but she hadn't quite been able to bring herself to read it. 'Yes, of course I did… It's in my handbag—'

'Good. I want you to read it…'

Fear took the place of desire on her face. 'Now?' she said, frowning anxiously. At his nod she slipped off the bed without another word.

She handled the heavy vellum fearfully, tracing her finger over Lorenzo's bold black writing. How was it that every time things were going well reality stuck its oar in and spoiled everything? She stood with her back to him so she could hide her feelings, but then, as if some internal starter gun had gone off inside her head, she ripped furiously at the envelope, pulling out the single sheet.

Her gaze, so well trained, so accustomed to studying each word in sequence to be sure she didn't miss anything important, hopped straight to the bottom of the page where Lorenzo had written the three most important words in the English language: I love you.

She stared at them unblinking for a while, standing motionless until it finally sank in, and then, returning to the beginning of the letter, she read it through. When she'd finished she held the sheet to her chest, and then pulled it away again to read it through once more. She was terrified as she began reading that the words might have changed, or disappeared; that they might be nothing more than a figment of her imagination. But they were still there: I love you; signed, Lorenzo.

He loved her? Lorenzo loved her?

'I'm so sorry,' she whispered, turning to face him. 'If I'd

had any idea... If I hadn't been such an idiot after the interview, I'd have read this and saved us both a lot of trouble...'

Lorenzo had resigned from the scholarship project, but had decided to continue his career at the bar in London. He was asking her to stay with him whatever she decided to do in life, but he asked her to think about the future very carefully and not to hurry into anything.

'So many thoughts in your eyes,' Lorenzo observed quietly. 'Are you going to share any of them with me?'

'I love you too...more than anything in the world.'

'And you're not hurting too badly because of the scholarship?'

'The scholarship? No.' She had almost forgotten it. It was behind her now, and only the shadow of her parents' disappointment remained.

'And the future?' Lorenzo prompted her.

She did have an idea what she would like to do, but every time she thought about it her mother's face flashed into her mind.

'You must have thought about it.'

'I have...' And him. And his reaction when she told him. She wasn't sure she was ready to face that now. 'I think...'

'Yes?' he prompted.

'I think I don't want to think...' Her expression took on meaning.

'Well, I want you to think,' he said, still not coming any closer. 'And I want you to share those thoughts with me. All I want is for you to be happy, and I know you well enough to know that drifting aimlessly through life isn't your style. To be happy you have to have a goal, Carly. You know that. You've always grasped the nettle in the past and made something good out of it. What's holding you back now?'

She knew what she wanted to do, but also knew it would

sound ridiculous when she told him. 'I love you, and that's enough.'

'Really?' His expression changed from sultry to sober in a heartbeat. 'Love takes more than words, Carly. It takes commitment and hard work. And you won't have the energy for that if you become bored, which, knowing you, I know you will. Look at your sister, Olivia—don't you think she longs to find something to do?'

'If law isn't for me I'm not sure I have the confidence after all these years of training to try anything else. It's a lot to give up—'

'Rubbish. I never heard such nonsense. If the past is holding you back it's time you moved on. Learn from it and then break free.' He paused for a moment and then said, 'Are you ready to share a glass of champagne?'

That was a loaded question, and everything hung on her reply.

CHAPTER SIXTEEN

CARLY CHOSE MARINATED goat's cheese with mandarin and honey-peppercorn dressing, followed by grilled swordfish with red pepper and fresh tomato coulis, while Lorenzo selected Thai-style rosti fish cakes, followed by Cajun-spiced tuna with cucumber crème fraîche, but then he ordered chocolate fondue for two with fresh dipping fruit...

'And champagne,' Carly reminded him.

'Are you sure?' His eyes were serious.

'Never more so...'

He placed the room-service order briskly and then dragged her into his arms. 'This is all I want, all I care about; you—' His voice was laced with passion, and as he kissed her champagne quickly became an afterthought, though he had ordered a second bottle to be kept on ice for them, just in case. 'We might need a few crates more,' he pointed out when she exclaimed at his extravagance. 'If you decide to take a bath in it...'

'Shall we leave that for the tabloids?' Carly suggested, wondering if she might burst with happiness.

'As long as we don't part with the hot chocolate sauce,' Lorenzo said wickedly.

'You read my mind again,' Carly said happily.

Lorenzo insisted on feeding her the best bits from his plate,

and the chocolate fondue was no exception, though he seemed
to be keeping most of it for himself. Not that she objected to
being a fruit plate. The peach was cool, the segments of
orange cooler still, and with a dribble of icy cold cream, aug-
mented by hot chocolate sauce and a sprinkling of nuts she
was nothing if not deliciously aroused.

There wasn't a part of her to be left neglected, Lorenzo
declared, and he was as thorough as he had promised to be,
right down to the swathes of towels he made her lie on while
he ministered to her needs on the bed. Her clothes were scat-
tered round the floor, as were his. Her body was in raging
torment for him, but he refused to hurry. She must learn to be
patient, he insisted, slipping one of her legs over his shoulders. He was going to finish every scrap of the chocolate
sauce, he assured her, dribbling it in a warm stream onto her
most sensitive, her most secret place.

Not a secret any more, at least, not to Lorenzo. She had
never felt a sensation like it. The insistent pressure of the
stream of chocolate, the rasp of Lorenzo's tongue and the heat
of his breath, the rhythmic sucking motion of his lips; sensation didn't come any better than this, and yet every time she
drew close he drew back.

'Are you determined to send me mad?'

'Haven't I taught you anything about the benefits of
delay?" he countered, licking chocolate off his lips as he
stared down at her.

'You have a very healthy appetite,' Carly observed, moving restlessly as Lorenzo examined the fruit bowl to see
what was left.

'And I love apple, in particular. It's so firm and juicy,' he
said, doing incredible things with it.

She bucked towards him as he continued his experiments
with the fruit salad. 'You can't leave me like this,' she com-

plained when every piece of fruit had been eaten, and Lorenzo paused to wipe his hands on a hot towel. 'I might die of frustration.'

'Somehow I doubt that,' he said with a confidence that raised her to new levels of arousal. 'So you want me?' he said.

'Don't tease me, Lorenzo, you know I do.'

His wicked gaze challenged her. 'Show me…'

Drawing her knees back, she offered herself to him.

'Tell me…'

She begged him to take her in words she hardly recognised, begged him to ease the ache inside her where she needed him to be, so firm and hard and strong. He came to her then, and she writhed beneath him, inviting him on. He took control, his strong hands positioning her; one cradled her buttocks, while the other cupped her face, holding for his first impassioned, love-hungry kiss. The time for subtlety had long passed and now desire overtook them.

Lorenzo's first thrust sank deep. It was a raw display of sexual power and sexual need that filled and stretched her, and sent them both to the very edge right away, but as he knew this he withdrew slowly…withdrew completely. She whimpered her complaint, and so, with his lazy, confident smile tugging at the corners of his mouth he took her very slowly again. He went as deep as he could, taking his time to allow her to relish every moment, until every muscle and nerve ending she possessed was mad for more. 'Faster,' she begged him hoarsely. 'Faster now…'

Lorenzo's answer was to repeat the sensation-packed stealth invasion again and again until she couldn't remain still beneath him a second longer. Lifting her hips towards him, she claimed him greedily, drawing him deep into the heart of her womb where she held him with powerful muscles until he obeyed her wishes. Pulling out, he thrust firmly, once, twice, and then in a gloriously rhythmical pattern at a much brisker pace.

'More…more,' she begged, working her body in the same rhythm as his. She craved fulfilment, but wanted it to last for ever. Lorenzo ground his hips against her to heighten her pleasure, while she clung to him in desperation until ecstasy claimed her. She was only dimly aware as she called out wildly that her abandoned cries had mingled with those of Lorenzo.

Each time they made love it was a revelation, Carly reflected drowsily as she lay safe in Lorenzo's arms. They had showered, made love again and now they were sleeping together. She loved him, she loved everything about him. She loved his body and loved his mind. The feel of his naked flesh beneath her hands was addictive; the slide of muscle, the shift of limbs, the sheer weight of him and the power he exuded. Not to mention his finesse, Carly thought with pleasure, listening to her body's quiet satisfaction. Lorenzo was magnificent, and he had put himself and all his skills at her disposal. What more could she ask? Gazing at him as he sprawled in contentment at her side, she had to confess he was even more beautiful than she had imagined when they first met. Perfectly proportioned, he was steel to her cushioned softness; they fitted perfectly together, and for the first time in her life her generous curves made sense. When she pressed her lips against his chest she could feel his heart beating steadily and strong; he was her anchor, her port in a storm…

Carly wasn't sure how long she slept, but she woke to find Lorenzo on one elbow at her side, looking down at her. He brushed the tangles of hair from her face.

'I enjoy watching you sleep.'

She made a sound of contentment. 'I don't know how you're still awake when every inch of me is exhausted. Where do you find the strength?'

'You're my inspiration?' he said dryly.

But there was a look in his eyes she hadn't seen before. 'What are you thinking about, Lorenzo?'

'I heard you talking to your mother in the kitchen. I have good hearing and plenty of practice at speaking while I listen. I heard her ask you if you might be pregnant.'

'Well, I'm not.'

'Can you be sure?'

They'd just made love unprotected, so, no, she couldn't be sure.

'Would you be disappointed if you found that you were not pregnant?' Lorenzo asked her.

She didn't want children…of course, she didn't. The only thing she had ever wanted before Lorenzo came along was a career… All her mother had ever wanted for her was a career, Carly amended silently. She had a major rethink on her hands.

Lorenzo pressed her for an answer.

'I'd be disappointed,' she admitted softly.

'You can have it all,' he said. 'You do know that, don't you? Career, family—'

She gave herself a warning, knowing she couldn't even begin to face the pain if she talked herself into believing Lorenzo wanted a family with her.

'Yes, but as I'm not pregnant—'

'We can soon put that right—'

'Lorenzo—'

'Are you complaining?'

'No,' she gasped.

'Happy Christmas, baby…'

It took everything she'd got to open one eye, and then Carly saw that Lorenzo was not only up and about, he was shaved, dressed, and ready to hit the road.

'Half an hour and the driver will be here,' he reminded her. 'You'd better get up.'

'Must I?' She brushed the hair out of her eyes to look at him.

'Unfortunately, yes.'

She swung her reluctant limbs over the side of the bed. 'Merry Christmas, Lorenzo…' She had barely enough strength left to form the words. 'I think you drained every ounce of energy out of me last night.'

'I'm sure there's plenty more where that came from. I only wish we could stay longer and find out,' he said, folding her in his arms, 'but we have a take-off slot to fill.'

'Okay,' Carly murmured reluctantly, snuggling close. Winding her arms around his neck, she turned her face up for a kiss, and then complained when Lorenzo lifted her out of bed and steered her towards the bathroom.

'It's lucky that one of us has some self-control,' he said.

'Yours wasn't so hot last night.'

'That was a one-off,' he assured her. 'Go on,' he urged, 'I won't relent.'

Good, Carly thought with satisfaction, leaning back against the closed door. And wasn't that what she loved about him, the challenge, the wall to kick against? But what if her mother was proved right? What if Lorenzo was just using her for sex? No. He loved her. She firmed her jaw. Lorenzo loved her.

'Don't take too long,' he called through the door. 'We can't miss that slot.'

'Move in here,' Lorenzo suggested when they got back to his apartment.

'Are you serious?' Carly stared at him.

'Why not? What's the point in keeping a room at Louisa's when you're going to be here with me? I'm going to have to put a lot of time and effort into satisfying your demands, and I'll need you on site for that.'

The way Lorenzo was talking made living together sound like a building project. But maybe it was a project to him, something to carry out with his usual efficiency before finishing it and walking away... Giving him chance to start again on a fresh *project*. Carly's heart squeezed tight as she thought about it. 'You mean like a temporary arrangement?'

'Carly...' Lorenzo's lips tugged up at one corner as he shook his head. His thumbs were lodged in his belt loops with his fingers pointing the way to an impressive bulge, which took her mind off...everything.

As they ripped clothes off she couldn't help noticing his socks were covered in rabbits. 'Are these prophetic?' she said, laughing as she tugged them off.

'What do you think?' Lorenzo demanded, throwing her down onto the bed.

'I think you'd better show me.'

'My pleasure,' he said.

'Mine,' Carly argued with a gasp.

'You have a real talent for making me forget everything,' she said much later, turning her head on the pillows to look at Lorenzo.

'I've had years of practice in court—but I haven't succeeded in making you forget everything, have I, Carly?'

She sighed as he stroked her breasts.

'There's still all this hurt inside you...'

'Hurt?' Capturing his hand, she held it in place. 'If you mean that visit home, I'm over it. I'm made of stronger stuff than you seem to think.' His face assumed the masklike quality she recognised from court. 'I can't thank you enough for flying me up there.'

'You don't need to thank me.'

'And I'm not hurting,' she assured him.

He had only done what anyone with the means would do for someone they loved. Had no one ever made a gesture to Carly before that wasn't connected to the advancement of her career? Perhaps her father and sister were frightened to. The treats and surprises his parents had heaped on him made him realise how lucky he'd been and he wanted that for Carly. 'Let's get up and take a shower,' he suggested, 'and then we'll open our Christmas presents.'

'Presents plural?' she said, already sounding worried. 'But I only got you one—' Her cheeks reddened.

'You're my present; the only present I want.' He would drum that guilt out of her however long it took. He raced her to the shower, giving her a head start, and she shrieked with excitement as he closed in. Her eyes were already darkening in anticipation as he shut the doors. She was in his arms with her legs locked around his waist before the water had turned warm, and this time her shrieks came fast and furious and had nothing to do with the temperature of the water.

'And you call me insatiable,' he said.

'The more I get, the more I want,' she admitted.

'Love can do that to you,' he said.

'Love…'

'Don't tell me you're just using me for sex,' he teased her

Her anxiety dissolved into a cheeky smile. 'Now there's an idea…'

It was some time before they emerged from the bathroom swaddled in warmed towelling robes. He had to carry Carly because his spare robe was far too big for her. He had to carry her anyway, because he wanted to. 'We'll get dressed, and then have presents,' he said, ignoring her complaint. If they didn't get dressed soon, Christmas would never happen. 'And if we don't hurry up we'll miss supper—'

'Supper out on Christmas Day?'

'A friend of mine has opened a restaurant. It's open, and he's saving us a table.'

'You were pretty confident I'd come back here with you.'

'You should know from court I always plan ahead.' He dipped his head to look her in the eyes. 'And I never doubted it…'

Carly gulped when she saw how many carrier bags Lorenzo had hidden behind the sofa. 'These can't all be for me!'

'I wasn't hanging around to edit the contents. Half an hour in that place was enough for me.'

Lorenzo shopping? Now she understood. 'So where do I start?'

'With the underwear—that's usual, isn't it?'

The ribbon-trimmed box from her favourite store was unmistakable, the contents racier and more expensive than she would ever have dared choose. Plus Lorenzo seemed to have taken one of everything—in pink, in aquamarine, and in…gulp!

'For when you're feeling frisky. Shall we move on to the outer casing?'

Which just happened to be the softest cashmere dress in pale caramel, which he'd teamed with knee-high suede boots in a slightly darker shade. The heels could most safely be described in polite society as wicked in the extreme. 'Oh, Lorenzo, they're fabulous,' Carly exclaimed, trying them on.

'And there's a jacket.' He angled his chin towards the remaining carrier bag.

'You shouldn't have bought me all this. It must have cost you a fortune.'

'Won't you try it on?'

Carly was speechless. She had never bought clothes of this quality for herself.

'If you don't like anything you can change it. I won't be offended,' Lorenzo assured her.

'I don't want to change a thing,' she said, finding her voice. Everything was just perfect, and in the classic styles with a quirky edge she looked almost fashionable.

'You'd look beautiful in a sack,' Lorenzo argued.

'If you don't mind I'll pass on the sack and stick with the clothes you bought me.' She leaned back against him and sighed. 'Honestly, Lorenzo, I don't know what to say… I'm overwhelmed.'

'Say you're happy; say you believe me when I tell you you're beautiful…' Clasping her shoulders in his warm hands, he nuzzled her hair out of the way and planted a kiss on her neck.

'But—'

'No buts…' Turning her to face him, he silenced any remaining doubts she might have had with a kiss.

Lorenzo was wonderful, and she loved him with all her heart, but what would he say when she told him her dreams for the future?

'You're doing it again,' he said.

'What am I doing?'

'Thinking too much…' He looked at her seriously for a moment and then his lips tugged up, 'Do I get my present now?'

He'd taken the parcel out of his mailbox and it was sitting on the coffee-table. 'It's nothing compared to all this,' she said, gesturing around.

'If you chose it I'll love it, just as I love you…' He kissed her hand as he spoke, and then, turning it, kissed her palm too.

He loved her. She would never get used to it. Did he love her? In her head her mother huffed.

Lorenzo ripped the paper off her gift and then sat staring at the book she'd bought him.

'How did you know?' he said at last. 'How did you know that Frank Frazetta is one of my all-time favourite artists?'

'Call it an educated guess.' But it was more than that. Frank Frazetta was a famous American artist who drew fantasy heroes and larger-than-life battle scenes. He idealised the fight for right, and celebrated heroes and heroic principles, and in her opinion every one of Lorenzo's dragon-slaying qualities existed between the pages of that book.

She looked over Lorenzo's shoulder as he turned the pages depicting another man's incredible flights of imagination. Some people might think the images off the wall, but Frazetta had been a student of anatomy, and was an impressive artist in every way. His work seemed a perfect match for Lorenzo. Wasn't he off the wall with his austere front, his sensual nature, and his crazy-coloured socks?

'It's a perfect gift,' he said in a way that made her heart clench.

But it was more than that for him, Lorenzo realised as he stared into Carly's eyes. She had reached into his soul and plucked something out of there. In a way he wasn't even surprised she'd bought him the book of illustrations; they were like two sides of the same coin. Frank Frazetta had been his late father's favourite artist too. 'While there are men like this around,' he used to say, stabbing a work-worn finger at one of the illustrations, 'everything will be okay. You gotta be like them, Lorenzo. In here…' He'd thump his chest at that point. It was a regular Sunday night routine to prepare them both for the rigours of the week ahead—his at the private school, and his father at the meat factory where he worked to pay the fees.

'Do you really like it?' she said.

He realised Carly must think him distant, when nothing could be further from the truth. 'You have no idea what this little book means to me,' he assured her.

CHAPTER SEVENTEEN

'I LOVE IT.' Lorenzo put the book in pride of place on the coffee-table. 'You couldn't have bought me anything I'd like more.'

When he'd stopped kissing her Carly asked what time they had to be at the restaurant. 'Soon, but first I want to know what you've decided about the future.'

'You'll think me silly…'

'Try me…'

She gazed at his socks, sombre blue, decorated with the scales of justice. Somehow that made it harder to tell him, but she couldn't put it off for ever. 'Not law,' she said.

She waited, but Lorenzo didn't cut in as she had expected him to. 'I've had a wonderful training and a wonderful time at chambers. And it's all been worthwhile, because I wouldn't have met you if I'd chosen another path. So I have a lot to thank my mother for…'

He let that one pass. 'Well?' he said. 'What's it to be?'

'I'm going to be an event planner…'

Not, I want to be; I'm going to be. For once in his life he couldn't keep his mask in position. He knew she would eventually realize what he'd wanted her to. 'Carly, I'm delighted!' He swept her into his arms.

'You are?'

She looked amazed, but whatever the rest of the world thought of him he was a simple man with simple goals. He wanted to make a difference and raise a family, and to do that Carly had to be happy. What she'd just told him would finally bring her the sense of personal achievement that had proved so elusive in the past. 'I know you'll be fantastic. And if you get cards printed and circulate them amongst all the people who attended your Christmas party I'm sure you'll be snowed under with enquiries.'

'You really mean that, don't you?'

'I never say anything I don't mean. Now, come on, or we'll be late for Father Christmas—'

She shook her head. 'Don't tell me you're a believer?'

'Of course I am.'

As she laughed he made a silent pledge to fight each one of her demons in turn until there were no shadows left.

The restaurant Lorenzo took her to was a surprise. It was situated in something that looked more like an aircraft hangar than a glamorous eatery, and it was only when they walked inside and Carly smelled the food she realised why the huge space was packed out.

The smiling host had been waiting for them at the door, a man of similar age to Lorenzo, but with more dream than scheme in his dark blue eyes. He led the way for them through the tables.

'Don't be misled,' Lorenzo whispered discreetly in Carly's ear as they headed towards a generous-sized table overlooking the river. 'Tre's dreamy expression comes from his eternal quest for that coveted third Michelin star.'

'Can you read all my thoughts?' Carly challenged him softly.

'Most of them,' he admitted. 'That's why I know we'll make such a good team.'

She had to try very hard not to read anything into that. 'This is really lovely,' she said as Lorenzo attracted the attention of the wine waiter.

'I thought it would make a nice change from Greasy Jo's,' he teased her.

'Don't remind me,' she protested, laughing. 'I'm never going to live that one down, am I?'

'Never,' Lorenzo assured her.

They both laughed.

He ordered champagne. 'You'll need a glass to toast Father Christmas,' he explained. 'And look... Here he is, right on cue...'

The celebrations allowed everyone to shed their inhibitions, Carly thought as Father Christmas wove his way through the tables; even she was excited.

The wine waiter filled her champagne flute to the brim, and reaching across the table, Lorenzo found her hand and linked their fingers together. 'I just hope you like your gift.'

'I'm sure I will.' She had seen some of the other women opening packages that contained a beautiful orchid in a tiny glass vase. The men's gifts appeared to be miniature tins of coffee beans, which she knew Lorenzo would love. 'But mine's different to everyone else's gift.' It was a lot smaller, and Lorenzo had a different gift too.

'I get a personal gift from Tre because we've known each other so many years,' he explained. 'He can never resist his annual dig at my fashion sense.'

'So you get socks?' Carly guessed.

'That's right,' Lorenzo confirmed. 'And what do you make of this one?' he said as Father Christmas left the smaller gift in front of Carly.

'Why would Tre buy me something when we don't even know each other?'

'Who said Tre bought it for you?'

'You said— No, you didn't,' Carly amended.

'For a moment there I really thought all those years of legal training had been wasted,' Lorenzo said dryly.

'Can I open it?'

'After me.' He was already ripping the Christmas paper off his socks.

'Reindeer socks with bells on?' Carly laughed. 'At least I'll hear you coming.'

'Why don't you open yours now?'

There was a tiny jewellery box beneath the Christmas paper. Possibilities raced through Carly's mind—collar studs? This was embarrassing. She had only just told Lorenzo about her intention to leave law and now it looked as if he had bought her something she would use in court: collar studs, or cufflinks engraved with the crest of her inn of court, perhaps—they were very popular. 'You shouldn't have,' she said awkwardly.

'How do you know what it is until you open it?' he pointed out.

Maybe it was a joke present. She went hot and cold at the thought that she might have made a fool of herself confessing her love for Lorenzo, just as her mother had predicted. But he'd said he loved her. He did love her. She firmed her resolve, and, pressing the catch, released the lid.

'Well?' Lorenzo said as she sat in silence. 'What do you think?'

She wasn't capable of thinking, or speaking, or anything else at the moment. She was too busy staring in disbelief at the biggest solitaire diamond she'd ever seen. 'Is this thing real?'

'No, it's glass. I got it out of a cracker,' Lorenzo observed dryly. 'Now would you like to try it on?'

'But what's it for?' All her brain cells had collided in a heap and the ring was firing all the colours of the rainbow at her, confusing the issue.

'What's it for?' Lorenzo repeated. 'Now, let me think... Maybe it's a bonus for good behaviour? No—' he shook his head '—you don't deserve that. You've been extremely naughty over these past few days. For good work, then?' His lips pressed down. 'Well, that can't be right, because you haven't started your new job yet—'

'Lorenzo!'

'Carly.' Angling his head, he stared at her with exasperation. 'For someone with so much brain power you have precious little common sense. Why can't you just accept that I love you, and that I want to be with you for ever? I want to marry you. I *want* to buy you a diamond ring.'

'And what Lorenzo wants Lorenzo gets?' Carly's face started to relax into a smile.

'Something like that,' he admitted.

'Are you sure it's for me?'

'Unless you have an invisible friend?' He stared over her shoulder.

'Lorenzo...'

'Give the ring to me,' he instructed.

She gave him the box with the ring still intact. She couldn't believe such a fabulous piece of jewellery was destined to find its home on her finger. She was already braced for the punchline and the laughter. If Lorenzo mentioned crackers one more time she would—

'I'm surprised you can't recognise a Tiffany box—'

'A Tiffany box?' she said. 'Let me see that again...'

She held out her hand, but he just laughed. 'I can see I have a lot of educating to do. Now hold out your hand, Ms Tate...'

The ring fitted perfectly.

'Do you like it?'

Carly studied the fabulous diamond on her wedding finger. 'I don't know what to say.'

'Say you love me—say you'll marry me…'

'You do mean it, don't you?'

Lorenzo took hold of her hand. 'Don't you know how much I love you yet? Don't you know how much I want to marry you?' His lips tugged up in a wicked grin. 'Don't you know how much I want to make babies with you? I thought I'd made at least that much clear. Seems I'll have to put in a lot more time convincing you…'

'I will marry you, Lorenzo—' She broke off.

'Are you all right?' He was instantly concerned as she swayed a little in her seat.

'It's just the shock,' Carly explained. 'I felt a little faint…'

'Can you describe your feelings exactly?' Lorenzo said, staring at her intently.

'Lorenzo,' she reminded him, 'we're not in court now.'

'My mother felt strange every time, and she had seven of us.'

'Your mother? Lorenzo, please, whatever's wrong with me, it has nothing to do with whatever your mother suffered seven times.'

'How can you be so sure?'

She looked at him and then at the ring. 'Because anyone would faint with shock when they saw the size of this diamond.'

'Oh, come now, Carly,' Lorenzo argued dryly. 'There isn't a woman alive who would faint at the size of a diamond—unless it was tiny, of course.'

CHAPTER EIGHTEEN

It was some weeks before Lorenzo had the opportunity to tell Carly, 'I told you so,' and nine months before he held their beautiful daughter, Adriana, in his arms. He brought his two girls home from hospital to the country house he and Carly had chosen together in the latter stages of Carly's pregnancy. The Georgian manor house was reminiscent of the boutique hotel in Cheshire where their baby had almost certainly been conceived. The property was an easy drive from the city, and provided them both with a much-needed break from the hustle and bustle of city life. An Internet connection had been set up to ensure that the newest party planner in town could continue to grow her business while heavily pregnant, or nursing a baby, and Carly's inbox was already bulging with an impressive number of potential clients.

She was integral to his life in every way, and his only concern was her happiness. He had settled effortlessly into the role of devoted husband, and now devoted father, and, following in the footsteps of his parents, he was determined to share that happiness around.

'My mother won't come,' Carly stated confidently six weeks after the birth of Adriana, by which time he judged her ready to face the storm. 'She'll never forgive me for leaving law.'

'We'll see, shall we?' When had he ever allowed a small thing like a mother-in-law to put him off his stride?

'Who said your mother wouldn't come?'

Carly couldn't believe her eyes as her father's car pulled into the yard. Livvie piled out first, and then her father hurried round to open the passenger side door.

'Mother?' she breathed incredulously.

'And bearing gifts, by the look of it,' Lorenzo observed, watching as Mrs Tate marshalled her handbag, her carrier bags and her troops.

'She looks lost,' Carly said, staring transfixed through the window. Her father and Livvie were hurrying excitedly up the path, while her mother remained in the same spot, gazing up at the façade of Carly and Lorenzo's beautifully restored home.

'She *is* lost,' Lorenzo pointed out. 'She's not in her kingdom now, she's in yours.'

'I've got to go to her…'

Lorenzo's voice stopped Carly halfway across the hall. 'Take it easy,' he said. 'Don't intimidate her—'

'Intimidate my mother?'

'Just remember the tables have been turned, Mrs Domenico. Be gentle with her…that's all I'm saying.'

Carly's face softened as she looked at Lorenzo holding their baby. He was such an amazing man. 'You know I will…'

'Yes, I do. That's why I love you.'

'I love you too…'

As Carly opened the door Livvie fell into her arms, hugging her as if she would never let her go. 'Can I hold the baby?' she asked the moment they released each other.

Lorenzo made the careful transfer, and then went to greet Mr Tate. Giving the older man a firm handshake, he drew him into the house as if they were old friends. 'Your father and I have things to discuss,' he said to Carly as father and daughter hugged, 'so you can't keep him long.'

'My flying lesson,' Carly's father confided. 'Good man. He remembered.' Holding Carly's face between his hands, he searched her eyes. 'That's better,' he said quietly, releasing her.

As Lorenzo led him away towards the kitchen, and Livvie followed with baby Adriana, Carly waited with apprehension to greet her mother. She felt anxious, but she told herself she couldn't possibly feel half as awkward as her mother.

'Carly…'

The voice hadn't changed, and they didn't attempt to embrace each other.

'Come in…' Carly stood back, remembering Lorenzo's counsel. 'Welcome…'

'Very nice,' her mother observed, walking past her. 'You've done very well for yourself, Carly.'

Lorenzo always made her feel that he had done very well for himself too, but the moment her mother spoke the doubts set in again. As she turned and raked her face with the narrowed gaze, searching for signs of insecurity, it took all she'd got to respond openly with a smile. 'Won't you come into the kitchen? Everyone's there.'

'Don't rush me, Carly. I bought you something.' She pushed a carrier bag into Carly's hands. 'I expect you've got something better. It's only a quilt cover for the baby's cot.'

'But it's beautiful,' Carly exclaimed softly as she looked inside the bag. 'I love it. Thank you.'

'Your father chose it,' her mother said awkwardly. 'And we bought a little gift for Lorenzo too, which I chose.'

Carly hid her astonishment. 'That's very generous of you, and there was absolutely no need.'

'There was every need,' her mother argued. 'This is Lorenzo's house, and we're enjoying his hospitality.'

Carly nodded. The barb might sting, but she refused to let it show.

'Well, go on…look at them,' her mother urged impatiently, handing over a small stiff bag. 'You'd better make sure I got it right.'

'I'm sure you did,' Carly reassured. When she looked inside the bag she had to try very hard indeed not to laugh. Her mother's gift to Lorenzo was socks. Grey socks. It would take more than that to turn Lorenzo into a strawberry cream, Carly reflected, pressing her lips down hard to keep from smiling. 'They're lovely,' she said. 'And it was very kind of you to think of it.' Her mother didn't seem such a dragon any more, and impulsively she leaned forward and kissed her on the cheek.

Her mother jerked back as if she'd been hit. 'I'm not interested in whether you like them or not. What I want to know is will Lorenzo like them? We'd better keep on his right side. You'll need someone to support you now you've thrown away your career.'

'And got another one,' Carly reminded her mother, who responded with a cynical hum. 'I'm sure he'll love the socks,' she lied, for the sake of her mother's feelings.

'This way, is it?' her mother said briskly, turning away.

'That's right.' And don't stop walking until you find the tall, dark handsome man wearing jeans, a rugby shirt and ruby-red, heart-festooned socks, Carly thought happily. For the first time in her life her mother couldn't hurt her; in fact she felt sorry for her and for everything they'd missed over the years. Lorenzo was right; her mother was far more vulnerable in this situation than she was.

Carly followed her mother into the kitchen where she found her hovering just inside the door. It was as if she couldn't bring herself to walk into the room, which was strange, Carly thought, because she found the scene idyllic. There was home-cooked food on the table, and the people she loved were standing around it. Her very own newborn baby was lying contented and asleep in her sister's arms…

Lorenzo found her gaze and smiled reassurance at her. His look told her how much he loved her, and how he was always there for her, whatever might happen.

'Won't you come and join us, Mother?' Carly said, returning to the door where her mother was still standing. Taking her mother's arm, she drew her gently inside the room.

Lorenzo came forward and put his arm round her shoulders. As he did so Carly noticed her mother's gaze flinch away and land on Olivia…with disapproval. She'd never seen that before. Her mother started to say something and then stopped herself. As she looked at Carly's father for support her mouth hardened when she realised he was too engrossed in his grandchild to notice her.

'Support the baby's head, Olivia,' she said, her voice sounding cracked and strained. 'Olivia, are you paying attention?'

'Of course I am, Mother,' Livvie crooned, gazing adoringly at her niece. 'Don't you think she's lovely?'

'What do I think? Does anyone care what I think?' When this received no answer, Mrs Tate went on. 'I think it's hard to credit Carly got married before you and had a baby.' The harsh words were out, but somehow they'd lost their sting; everyone was too happy to take it in. 'You'd better hurry up and find a man, Olivia,' she pressed on, 'or all the best ones will be gone.' She flashed a meaningful glance at Lorenzo.

'Olivia is taking her time to pick out the best of the best. Isn't that right, Livvie?' Lorenzo said kindly, and perhaps only Carly detected the thread of disapproval in his gaze as he looked at her mother, but then she knew his court mask.

'Well, she'd better hurry up, that's all I've got to say—'

'Mother—' Carly began, noticing that Livvie was now paying attention and was on the verge of tears.

'Your mother always did have to have the last word,' her father cut in to everyone's surprise. 'Me? I've always known what a lucky man I am to have two exceptional daughters.'

'Well said, Mr Tate,' Lorenzo agreed.

'Call me Arthur. And now you and I had better discuss that flying lesson—'

'What?' Exploding out of her brooding silence, Mrs Tate clutched her chest.

'Don't worry, Enid, I won't be taking you with me,' Carly's father said dryly.

There was another moment of silence, and then Carly noticed her mother was blinking back tears. She was about to go to her when her mother looked at her beseechingly. 'Can *I* hold her?'

There was such hope and fear in her voice it was as if the world as Carly knew it had come to an end, and something far better had taken its place. 'Of course you can,' she said warmly.

Olivia carried her baby niece across the room and placed her carefully in her grandmother's arms. 'Adriana, meet Granny,' Carly said softly, smiling at Livvie and Lorenzo before backing away.

'Thank you.' Her mother's gaze flickered up, and then quickly flashed back to her grandchild.

As she was the child of two such strong-minded parents it came as no surprise to anyone that Adriana had her own thoughts on reconciliation. Curling her tiny fist around her grandmother's forefinger, she held on tight.

'This is a new beginning,' Carly's mother murmured, entranced.

'Yes, well, let's hope so,' Carly's father commented. 'Are you coming, Lorenzo? Your study, didn't you say? I think we can safely leave the ladies in peace now.'

Lorenzo shot a look at Carly as if to say this division of the sexes wasn't their way, but for a day, if it made her parents happy, it would be worth it.

Carly put her arm around Livvie's shoulders as they watched their mother with Adriana. 'Your turn next,' she whispered. 'That's if you want a baby.'

'Perhaps I'd better find a man first?' Livvie suggested.

'Good idea,' Carly agreed, sharing a smile with her sister.

Later that night Lorenzo suggested they leave everyone to it. Adriana had so many nursemaids her parents were superfluous for once. He didn't wait for an answer before drawing his beloved wife out of the room.

'You worked a miracle today,' he told Carly, 'and I'm proud of you.'

'You worked the miracle,' she argued.

'Can we agree just this once to reach a compromise?' Lorenzo suggested, starting to unbutton her blouse. 'I think the miracle is Adriana…'

'Well, I'm not going to argue with you about that…'

Easing her head back to give Lorenzo better access to her neck, Carly knew that arguing was the last thing on her mind now, though there was definitely a storm brewing—of the most tempestuous and physical kind.

'Your breasts are enormous,' Lorenzo approved as if he'd never seen them before. 'I adore them…' Casting her bra aside, he swung her into his arms. 'Shall we?' he invited, moving towards the bed.

'Only if you take your socks off.'

'I'm not sure I can wait that long.'

But they did take his socks off—they took every single piece of clothing off.

'We don't always make it this far,' Carly said, laughing as

Lorenzo lowered her down onto the bed. 'Do you think the fire is dying down?'

Taking hold of her hand, he placed it over the throbbing proof of his continued interest. 'I'm not sure,' he said. 'What do you think?'

'I think I need regular reminders,' she told him wickedly.

He raked his stubble against her neck in the way he knew she liked, but when she reached for him he told her, 'Be patient… Haven't I taught you anything?'

'So much, I hardly know where to start.'

'Fortunately, I do,' he said, muffling her cries with kisses until she grew frantic underneath him. Carly's appetite was a source of constant pleasure to him, and he never tired of giving her the satisfaction she craved. Watching pleasure unfold on her face was one of his greatest joys in life. She was fierce in bed, demanding and passionate, and she was the mother of his child, sweet, kind and loving. She was the lynchpin of his family around which everything else revolved. 'I love you, Carly Tate.'

'Carly Domenico,' she corrected him in the scant few seconds he allowed her before finding another way to silence her.

Later, when she had quietened, he told her about the plans he'd made. 'I've taken an island for a month—'

'Of course you have,' she said, stroking his face.

'No, really, I have…'

'Are you serious?'

'Never more so. I'm going to fly the wife I adore and our baby, along with Adriana's nurse, to a tiny Caribbean island where my beautiful wife can lie in the sun all day and dream about…me.'

Carly laughed. 'You're impossible.'

'We've already established that,' Lorenzo said, kissing her into submission. 'And, of course, for this trip my wife will need some new clothes...' He reached beneath the bed for the parcel he'd put there earlier. 'For instance, she will need some new bikinis...' Reaching into the parcel, he showered some vivid scraps of fabric down on her. 'And, of course, she will require this season's must-have, ridiculously impractical underwear—'

'But, Lorenzo, I'm fat—'

'Carly, you have never been more beautiful in your life.' Bringing her hand to his lips, he planted a lingering kiss on her palm, staring into her eyes until she believed him.

'You are the most wonderful man in the world,' she whispered, 'and so generous. But, Lorenzo, I must buy something for you. What would you like?'

Her earnest expression made his lips curve in a smile. 'Isn't it obvious?'

'No...'

'How about socks?' he said wryly.

Celebrate 100 years of pure reading pleasure with Mills & Boon®

To mark our centenary, each month we're publishing a special 100th Birthday Edition. These celebratory editions are packed with extra features and include a FREE bonus story.

Now that's worth celebrating!

4th January 2008

The Vanishing Viscountess by Diane Gaston
With FREE story The Mysterious Miss M
This award-winning tale of the Regency Underworld launched Diane Gaston's writing career.

1st February 2008

Cattle Rancher, Secret Son by Margaret Way
With FREE story His Heiress Wife
Margaret Way excels at rugged Outback heroes...

15th February 2008

Raintree: Inferno by Linda Howard
With FREE story Loving Evangeline
A double dose of Linda Howard's heady mix of passion and adventure.

Don't miss out! From February you'll have the chance to enter our fabulous monthly prize draw. See special 100th Birthday Editions for details.

www.millsandboon.co.uk